TULIP IN THE DESERT

Muhammad Iqbal

Tulip in the Desert

A Selection of the Poetry of Muhammad Iqbal

edited and translated, with commentary and notes, by

MUSTANSIR MIR

Orient Longman

ORIENT LONGMAN LIMITED

Registered office
3-6-272 Himayatnagar, Hyderabad 500 029

Other offices
Bangalore, Bhopal, Bhubaneshwar, Calcutta, Chandigarh, Chennai
Ernakulam, Guwahati, Hyderabad, Jaipur, Lucknow
Mumbai, New Delhi, Patna

ISBN 81-250-1731-3

First published in India 2000
by arrangement with
C. Hurst & Co. (Publishers) Ltd., London

Printed in India by
Pauls Press, New Delhi 110020

Published by
Orient Longman Limited
1/24 Asaf Ali Road
New Delhi 110 002

For Talat

PREFACE AND ACKNOWLEDGEMENTS

Iqbal's poetry has such great variety that several anthologies of it could be compiled, each quite different from the others. The poems of this volume, while a personal selection, are representative of Iqbal's poetry, and their thematic arrangement reflects the diversity of subjects dealt with by Iqbal. Most of the poems are short (an anthology of Iqbal's longer poems is planned). The volume aims at introducing Iqbal's poetry to the English-speaking world in more than a perfunctory manner. While scholars and students will especially benefit from the detailed commentaries and notes, it is hoped that general readers in both Muslim and Western countries will find the work useful and interesting.

Many of the translations published here first appeared in the International Islamic University of Malaysia's *Research and Information Bulletin* (1993-5). A few of these were reprinted elsewhere, but without my approval. All published poems have been revised; others, freshly translated, have been included; and much new introductory and commentarial material has been added. In its present form and arrangement this is a new work.

Many people have encouraged me in this undertaking, and thanks are due to all of them, although I would like to single out three names: Dr Shabbir Akhtar, Dr Suheyl Umar, and Dr Mumtaz Ahmad. A fellowship at the Centre for Islamic Studies, Oxford, in 1995-6 enabled me to revise the work, and I am grateful for it. I thank Hurst & Co., the British publishers, for their superb editing. Finally, I am deeply grateful to Dr Ralph Russell, a foremost authority on Urdu language and literature, not only for his recommendation of the work but also for many valuable suggestions, from which I have benefited in making the final revision.

Youngstown State University
Youngstown, Ohio
June 1999

MUSTANSIR MIR

CONTENTS

ILLUSTRATIONS

NOTE ON TEXTS USED

The original texts used are *Kulliyyat-i Iqbal – Urdu* and *Kulliyyat-i Iqbal – Farsi*, both published in 1990 by the Iqbal Academy, Lahore, Pakistan. Poems are identified by the initials of the individual Persian or Urdu volumes in which they appear (see below). The Sheikh Ghulam Ali editions of the two sets of Urdu and Persian works (both 1973) are also cited, with page numbers given in square brackets. Thus, *BJ* 346 [298] means that the poem occurs in *Bal-i Jibril*, in *Kulliyyat-i Iqbal – Urdu*, 346 and 298 being the page numbers in the Iqbal Academy and Sheikh Ghulam Ali editions respectively. The abbreviated and full titles of the individual volumes in Iqbal's poetical works are:

Kulliyyat-i Iqbal – Urdu
- *AHU: Armaghan-i Hijaz – Urdu*
- *BD: Bang-i Dara*
- *BJ: Bal-i Jibril*
- *ZK: Zarb-i Kalaim*

Kulliyyat-i Iqbal – Farsi
- *AHF: Armaghan-i Hijaz – Farsi*
- *JN: Javid Namah*
- *PM: Payam-i Mashriq*
- *ZA: Zabur-i ᶜAjam*

INTRODUCTION

Muhammad Iqbal (1877-1938) is one of the pre-eminent writers of the Indian subcontinent, and the attention he has received from numerous writers, translators and critics in Western as well as Islamic countries testifies to his stature as a world literary figure. While his reputation is primarity as a poet, Iqbal has not lacked admirers for other reasons: he has been called 'the most serious Muslim philosophical thinker of modern times',[1] and the appellation 'poet-philosopher' has often been used. Here the hyphen is all-important: Iqbal's poetry and philosophy do not exist in isolation from each other, but are integrally related, his poetry serving as a vehicle for his thought. Iqbal wrote poetry in Urdu and Persian, and several volumes in each language exist. In the following pages a biographical sketch of Iqbal is followed by a brief treatment of some of the major themes and literary features of his poetry.

I

Iqbal was born in 1877 at Sialkot, a city in the present-day province of the Punjab in Pakistan. He received his early education in that city, where one of his teachers was Mir Hasan, an accomplished scholar with a knowledge of several Islamic languages. Mir Hasan gave Iqbal a thorough training in the rich Islamic literary tradition and influenced him deeply. Many years later (1922), when the British governor of the Punjab proposed to the British Crown that Iqbal be knighted in recognition of his literary achievements, Iqbal asked that Mir Hasan too should be awarded a title. When the governor remarked that Mir Hasan had not written any books, Iqbal replied that he, Iqbal, was the book Mir Hasan had produced. Mir Hasan received the title of *Shams al-'Ulama'* (sun of scholars).

For higher education Iqbal went to Lahore (1895), where he enrolled in Government College, obtaining his MA in philosophy

[1] Fazlur Rahman, *Islam*, 2nd edn (University of Chicago Press, 1979), 225.

in 1899. In Lahore, which was a major centre of academic and literary activity, Iqbal soon established his reputation as a poet. Among Iqbal's most admired teachers at Government College was Sir Thomas Arnold, and he in turn had great affection for Iqbal. Arnold helped Iqbal in his career as a teacher and encouraged him to undertake several research projects. When Arnold returned to England in 1904, Iqbal wrote a touching poem in which he expressed his resolve to follow him to England. Indeed Iqbal left to study at Cambridge the very next year. His choice of Cambridge was probably dictated by its reputation as a centre for the study not only of European philosophy but also of Arabic and Persian. During his three years' stay abroad, Iqbal obtained a BA from Cambridge (1906), qualified as a barrister at Lincoln's Inn in London (1906), and earned a PhD from Munich University (1908).

After returning to Lahore in 1908, Iqbal taught philosophy at Government College for a few years, but in 1911 he resigned from government service and set up his own legal practice – continuing meanwhile to write poetry in Urdu and Persian. His book *Asrar-i Khudi* (in Persian), published in 1915 and translated into English as *The Secrets of the Self* (1920) by Professor Reynold Nicholson of Cambridge, introduced Iqbal to the West. It was followed by several other volumes: *Rumuz-i Bikhudi* (1918), *Payam-i Mashriq* (1923), *Bang-i Dara* (1924), *Zabur-i ʿAjam* (1927), *Javid Namah* (1932), *Musafir* (1936), *Zarb-i Kalim* (1937), and *Armaghan-i Hijaz* (1938, posthumous). Iqbal also wrote prose: his doctoral thesis, *The Development of Metaphysics in Persia*, was published in 1908, and his *Reconstruction of Religious Thought in Islam* (with a seventh chapter added to the original set of six lectures, first published in 1930), in 1934. Many of Iqbal's poetical works have been translated into foreign languages, including English, German, Italian, Russian, Czech, Arabic and Turkish. His work has also given rise to a vast amount of critical literature in many languages.

Although his main interests were scholarly, Iqbal did not lack concern for the political situation of India and the fortunes of its Muslim community. Already in 1908, while in England, he had been chosen as a member of the executive council of the newly-established British branch of the Indian Muslim League. In 1931 and 1932 he represented the Muslims of India at the Round Table Conferences held in London to discuss India's future. And in 1930 he suggested in a lecture the creation of a separate homeland for the Muslims of India. Iqbal died in 1938, nine years before the creation of Pakistan, but it was his teaching that had been 'spiritually . . . the chief force behind the creation of Pakistan'.[2] He is Pakistan's national poet.

II

With the commentaries and notes provided in the following chapters there is no need for a detailed discussion here of the thematic and literary features of Iqbal's poetry. A few general points may, however, be made, mainly concerning the poems in this volume.

A reader of Iqbal's poetry is struck by its sheer thematic variety. Iqbal was deeply interested in the issues that have always exercised the best minds – the meaning of life, change and constancy, freedom and determinism, survival and progress, the relation between the body and the soul, the conflict between reason and emotion, evil and suffering, the position and role of human beings in the universe – and in his poetry he deals with these and other issues. He had also read widely in history, philosophy, literature, mysticism and politics, and developed catholic interests, and these are reflected in his poetry.

Iqbal celebrates humanity. On one level he shows broad acceptance of it. In 'The Story of Adam' (Chapter 4) the protagonist plays a variety of roles: as prophet, thinker, reformer, scientist, inventor, astronomer, martyr and iconoclast. In this poem Adam is not merely a religious figure belonging to a certain tradition, but represents the whole of humankind. On another level Iqbal takes pride in being human and has no desire to partake of the godhead of God (see Chapter 12, section 'The Human Being', subsection 'Being God and Being a Servant of God'). Human beings can hold their heads high because of their achievements in the world to which they were banished from paradise: if God made the night, then human beings made the lamp, and if God made deserts and mountains, human beings made parks and meadows ('A Dialogue Between God and Man', Chapter 1). Human beings must therefore strive to be perfect as human beings, and that is a goal they have yet to achieve.

[2] Ibid.

For Iqbal the theme of humanity is closely linked with the complex idea of *khudi* (literally 'selfhood'). Broadly, *khudi* represents the principle of the inner self combined with an urge to manifest itself. Societies as well as individuals have this quality, and it is on the development or suppression of one's *khudi* that success or failure in life depends; for example, the *khudi* of slaves is moribund. The aim of human beings should therefore be the recognition, discovery, cultivation, and assertion of their *khudi*. Iqbal's critique of Muslim societies is predicated on the assumption that they have lost their *khudi* or allowed it to become seriously impaired. The best source for an understanding of Iqbal's concept of *khudi* consists of the poems in which he discusses it (see Chapter 10, first five poems, and Chapter 12, section '*Khudi*').

Perfection – rather limitless perfection – is a motif that frequently recurs in Iqbal's poetry. In 'The Houri and the Poet' (Chapter 6), he says, 'I seek the end of what has no end', and 'In the spark I seek a star, in the star a sun'. Iqbal sees no end to human potential, and wants human beings to embark on a never-ending journey of discovery. To this end he emphasises the importance of constant action and perpetual movement as the only guarantee of survival in the world. Nations fall behind when they cease to be dynamic and start preferring a life of idle speculation to one of purposive action.

But the quest for perfection can give rise to irony. Indeed, human life is full of irony, for while human beings have been imbued with the desire to achieve perfection, they have been denied the ability to do so in practice. The first three poems of Chapter 4 – 'Man', 'Solitude', and 'The Dew and the Stars' – discuss several aspects of the irony of human life. The fourth and last poem, 'The Story of Adam', though ending on a more optimistic note, implies that human beings take a long time to discover the most important secret of existence.

'The heart has its reasons, of which reason is ignorant', says Pascal. Iqbal, who frequently tells of the conflict between head and heart, would agree, while adding that the conflict does not have to exist. Reason sometimes seeks to diminish the heart (or intuition), but both are essential to a harmonious life; ideally, the two should cooperate rather than clash (see Chapter 5).

Although his interests range widely, Iqbal essentially belongs to, and speaks from within, the Islamic tradition, employing for

[4]*I am . . . yours:* This statement is to be understood as a response to another – supposed to have been made by God. When Adam returns from the earth and stands in His court, God accuses him of making grave mistakes in his life. Adam replies: I admit I am at fault, but in spite of all my shortcomings and failures, I made the earth habitable in a way the angels were not able to, so look at my accomplishments and not at my failures. The phrase 'I am at fault' may also allude to Adam's first sin in Eden; 'and in a foreign land' refers to Adam being expelled to earth, where he is a 'foreigner'.

[5]*That stark . . . hardship:* The earthly world is beholden to its human resident for making it a wonderful place to live in. 'Gratefully remembers' is an idiomatic translation of *duᶜa'en deta hai*, literally 'It prays [for me]'. The connection between the literal and idiomatic meanings is that one prays for someone's well-being out of gratitude for the favours received from him.

[6]*An adventurous . . . ambush:* The reference is to paradise, where the poet now is. Paradise is an unexciting place because, representing perfection as it does, it has no room for anything new or adventurous. In a sense, then, the so-called imperfect world is better than paradise. Cf. 'The Houri and the Poet', Chapter 6.

[7]*The station . . . to it:* It is adventurous human beings who have undertaken to explore the earthly world. The angels (the word *qudsi* in the original means literally 'the holy ones') lack that courage which alone motivates the taking of grave risks in order to make new discoveries. Cf. couplet 5 of the last poem.

A DIALOGUE BETWEEN GOD AND MAN

GOD

I made the whole world with the same water and clay,
But you created Iran, Tartary, and Ethiopia.[1]
From the earth I brought forth pure iron,
But you made from that iron sword, arrow, and gun.
You made an axe for the tree in the garden,
And a cage for the songbird.

MAN

You made the night, I made the lamp;
You made the earthen bowl, I made the goblet.
You made deserts, mountains and valleys;
I made gardens, meadows and parks.
I am one who makes a mirror out of stone,[2]
And turns poison into sweet, delicious drink.[3,4]

PM 268-9 [284]

[1]*I made . . . Ethiopia:* i.e. I made a single world, but you carved it up into hostile lands; I created a single humanity, but you divided it into rival nations. The phrase 'water and clay' is equally applicable to the physical world (which is made of clay and water – or mortar and bricks, as one might say) and to human beings (whose constitutive elements are earth and water).

[2]*I am . . . stone:* I can transmute a hard, opaque substance into a delicate, bright object. There is possible wordplay in the use of the Persian words used for 'stone' and 'mirror' – *sang* and *ayina* – for, put in the construct state, they become *ayinah-i sang*, meaning 'crystal mirror'.

[3]*And turns . . . drink:* A reference to human achievements in fields such as medicine and chemistry.

[4]Man's argument in this poem is repeated by Iqbal in a quatrain (see Chapter 12, 'The Human Being', subsection 'A Creative Being', quatrain no. 1), where the human being is called a 'co-worker of God'.

2

PARADISE LOST AND REGAINED

On more than one occasion Iqbal expressed his wish to write poems in the style of John Milton, treating ostensibly the theme of the Fall of Man. His wish was not realised, but the poem 'Conquest of Nature' in *Payam-i Mashriq* might be regarded as the outline – or, in Milton's terminology, 'argument' – of the proposed work. In it Iqbal relates Adam's Fall and offers an interpretation of the story. The following summary leads to a fuller discussion of the poem.

The poem is in five parts. Part I speaks of the momentous event of Adam's birth. In the heavens there is much excitement and jubilation, but also concern and anxiety. The birth of a new creature possessing the freedom to think holds out a prospect of growth and achievement, but it also raises doubts and fears about the possible misuse of that freedom. The overall impression is that the universe is about to enter a new phase, and that nothing will ever be the same again. In Part II Iblis (Satan) defies God's command to pay homage to Adam, justifying himself on the grounds that his own constitutive element, fire, is superior to Adam's, which is earth. He claims to be the cause of all dynamism in the world and boldly predicts that Adam, though created by God, will eventually come over to his, Iblis's, side. In other words, Adam will pay homage to him and not he to Adam. In Part III Iblis tempts Adam by urging him to exploit his potential. He says that Adam must shake off his lethargy and start living a life of action, transforming himself from a meek pigeon into a fierce, bloodthirsty eagle. He exhorts Adam to get up and discover the world for himself, and promises to show him a new kingdom which he may rule if he shows sufficient courage. It is implied that Adam swallows Iblis's bait and will consequently be banished from his heavenly residence by God. In Part IV Adam leaves paradise. On first viewing the world that is to be his new home, Adam is fascinated; he relishes the thought of living a full life and discovering new things. In Part V Adam, on the Day of Judgment, argues before God that it was necessary for him to be ensnared by Iblis in order to be able to ensnare him in turn.

The 'Conquest of Nature' raises several intriguing issues and has some interesting literary features:

1. The story Iqbal tells is, of course, a religious story – a Qur'anic religious story. The birth of Adam, his seduction by Iblis and the scene of resurrection all give the story an Islamic setting and character. Yet 'The Conquest of Nature' is a highly original poem, especially in Iqbal's interpretation of the Fall of Adam. The poem is about a clash, or rather two clashes – one between Iblis and God and the other between Iblis and Adam. In the latter Adam emerges as the clear winner, thwarting Iblis's attempt to pit him against God. Iblis had wished Adam to follow him by disobeying God, but Adam, though taken in by Iblis and compelled to leave paradise, eventually realises that Iblis is not a friend but a foe, and the strategy he works out to defeat him is based on this understanding. Furthermore, while Iblis's defiance of God shows extreme arrogance, Adam presents his defence before God in all humility, acknowledging his fault. Adam's victory over Iblis is thus achieved on both moral and strategic grounds. And Iblis's defeat at the hands of Adam also becomes his defeat at the hands of God. Thus the outcome of the clash between Adam and Iblis determines the outcome of the clash between God and Iblis.

2. We mentioned Adam's strategy to defeat Iblis. Central to it is control of nature. Indeed, after a careful reading of the poem one realises that the title 'Conquest of Nature' itself alludes to the changing, or rather manifold, significance of nature in it. In Part I we learn that Adam's birth caused anxiety to nature, which was possibly apprehensive that a being endowed with a creative mind and critical eye would try to reduce it to subjection. It was not sure how to deal with such a being. In Part II Iblis identifies himself closely with nature, claiming that it owes its dynamism to him; he says that he is the force that binds the atoms together and governs the elements. In Part III Iblis invites Adam to come out of his paradisal hideout and conquer the world of nature. In Part IV Adam, on leaving paradise, expresses his fascination at making his first contact with nature. In Part V he argues that it was necessary for him to fall victim to Iblis's machinations, for this was the only way by which he could conquer nature – which,

in turn, was his only chance of bringing Iblis low. Nature thus figures in all five parts of the poem, but in each part it has a somewhat different significance. A comparison of Parts I and V brings out the difference most strikingly.

3. Adam's defence – namely that his commission of the sin was necessary to the fulfilment of the divine scheme – gives rise to a dilemma. If Adam had not sinned and had remained in paradise, Iblis would not have bowed down before him and thus God's command would not have been carried out. On the other hand, aiding in the fulfilment of the divine command would require that he sin, become a victim of Iblis, and then embark upon a course of action that would eventually bring Iblis to his knees. Which of the two would have been a better choice – a sinless Adam and an unfulfilled divine command or a sinful Adam and a divine command duly executed? Put differently, the question is: does the end justify the means? Iqbal discreetly refrains from answering it, leaving his readers to draw their own conclusions.

4. Does the poem have a message? It would seem that it does have one, deriving from Iqbal's interpretation of the story of Adam's Fall, and that the poem's title contains a clue to it. Iqbal seems to be saying that the only way in which Adam could have atoned for his lapse in paradise was through conquest of nature. The message of the poem is future-oriented, Iqbal taking a story of the past to chart a course of action for the future: control of nature – that was the dream Iblis showed to Adam, in order to mislead him, but that also was the means whereby Adam could redeem and rehabilitate himself. Conquest of nature thus affords Adam (it is important to remember that he represents humanity) an opportunity to turn his weakness into a strength; it is a kind of about-turn that would enable him to take the road back to paradise and become reconciled with God.

5. Notable in connection with Iqbal's proposed agenda of the conquest of nature is the role of *ʿaql* (both reason and the intellect). Adam in Part V speaks of *ʿaql-i kalan kar-i man* ('my *ʿaql*, doer of great deeds'), and the concluding couplet of the poem says that nature is conquered by the instrumentality of *ʿaql*, as a consequence of which Iblis is forced to bow down before Adam. Thus it is *ʿaql* which helps bring about the fulfilment of the divine command and the reinstatement of Adam in divine grace.

6. There are two apologies in the poem. In the first, in Part II,

Iblis seeks to justify his refusal to bow down before Adam, and in the second, in Part V, Adam seeks to justify his seduction by Iblis, but there is a fundamental difference between the two. Iblis persuades Adam to leave paradise by appealing to his ego and promising him domination over a fascinating world. But it is clear that, far from being Adam's well-wisher, Iblis is acting vengefully, for his secret wish is that Adam should become like him, which would be a victory for Iblis if it were to be fulfilled. Feeling humiliated by the command to abase himself before Adam, Iblis tries to lead him down the path of destruction and so defeat the divine plan, hoping thus to vindicate his refusal to bow down before a creature of dust. As Adam defends himself, he comes across as someone who would sacrifice himself for the sake of a noble cause. A manipulative and self-glorifying Iblis is thus contrasted with a magnanimous and altruistic Adam.

7. Adam's argument about the necessity of succumbing to Satan does sound somewhat specious, but he presents it only after falling into Satan's trap. The necessary consequences of the Fall had to be faced, but then there also had to be an attempt at redemption, and what Adam accomplished under the circumstances was remarkable.

8. The three major *personae* of the story are Adam, Iblis and God, but while Adam and Iblis speak, God does not. In Part II Iblis addresses God (who, it is implied, has already commanded him to bow down before Adam), and offers him a challenge: Adam, created by God, will in the end become a follower of Iblis. One feels that God is giving Iblis the silent treatment, but what does the silence really mean? In Part V Adam addresses God (who, it is implied, has already asked him to account for his lapse), and again God says nothing in response. One imagines (and hopes) that God would accept Adam's reasoning, but what would God actually say? The dramatic suspense of the poem is partly due to God's silence.

9. The poem demonstrates Iqbal's ability to tell a story effectively. Taking the entire span of human existence – from Adam's birth to his resurrection – as his temporal background, Iqbal selects five events in the story of Adam, telling a complete story. These five events represent all the crucial phases of the period in which Adam's destiny is played out (cf. the five-act structure of Renaissance and Elizabethan plays). The story has epic proportions. The whole

universe seems to have a stake in Adam's destiny: the great commotion in the heavens in Part I proclaims how fateful the event of Adam's birth is, and the tense atmosphere of Part V suggests that the outcome of his trial will have far-reaching repercussions.

10. Iqbal uses verbal links to establish a thematic and structural continuity in the poem. Especially notable are those between Part III and Part IV (in which, respectively, Iblis and Adam speak). Iblis describes a life of passion and longing as the ideal and Adam echoes that thought, using the same expression (*soz-o-saz*); Iblis calls paradise a 'trap' and Adam calls it a 'cage'; Iblis defines eternal life as *sokhtan-i na-tamam*, literally 'incomplete burning' or 'to burn away, without ever burning out', i.e. to have a constant longing for something, especially something unattainable, which thus impels one to greater efforts to achieve success; Adam uses similar words (*hamah soz-i na-tamamam*) to describe his own state. These and other links advance the plot of the story, and in Parts III and IV indicate also the extent to which Iblis has succeeded in 'brainwashing' Adam.

CONQUEST OF NATURE

I. THE BIRTH OF ADAM

Love exclaimed, 'Now one has been born
Who would roll his heart in blood!'[1]
Beauty trembled when she realised
That one with a penetrating look had been born![2]
Nature was distraught because,
From the dust of a world without will,
One had been born who could
Make and unmake himself,
And watch over himself.[3]
From the heavens the news went out
To eternity's sleeping-chamber:
'Beware, you who are veiled –
One has been born who will tear away all veils!'[4]
Desire, resting in the lap of life
And forgetful of itself,
Opened its eyes, and a new world was born.[5]
Life said, 'Through all my years
I lay in the dust and convulsed,
Until at last a door appeared
In this ancient dome'.[6]

II. IBLIS'S REFUSAL

I am not such a foolish angel
That I would bow to Adam!
He is made of dust, but my element is fire.[7]
It is my ardour that heats the blood
In the veins of the universe:
I am in the raging storm
And the crashing thunder;
I am the bond that holds the atoms together,
And the law that rules the elements;[8]
I burn[9] and give form –
I am the alchemist's fire.[10]

What I have myself made I break in pieces,
Only to create new forms from the old dust.
From my sea rises the wave
Of the heavens that know no rest[11] –
The splendour and glory of my element
Fashions the world.
The stars owe their existence[12] to You,
But they owe their motion to me:
I am the soul of the world,
The hidden life that is seen by none.
You give the soul to the body,
But I set that soul astir.
You rob on the highway by causing sloth,[13]
I guide along the right path with burning passion.[14]
I did not beg paupers to bow down before me[15]:
I am mighty, but do not need a hell;
I am a judge, but do not need resurrection.[16]
Adam – that creature of dust,
That short-sighted ignoramus –
Was born in your lap
But will grow old in my arms![17]

III. THE SEDUCTION OF ADAM

A life of passion and longing
Is better than eternal quiet,[18]
Even a dove that is caught in a trap,
But keeps flapping its wings,
Changes into an eagle.[19]
You do no more than bow down in humility;
Rise like the tall cypress tree, you who are slow to act!
The waters of Kawthar and Tasnim
Have robbed you of the joy of action.[20]
Take wine from the jug,
Real wine clear as crystal, made from grapes.[21]
'Good' and 'bad' are figments
Of the imagination of your Lord.

Take pleasure in action,[22]
Step out and and take what your desire.
Come, rise up, so that I may show you a new kingdom![23]
Open your eyes and go about
Seeing the sights the world has to offer.[24]
Now you are a drop of water worth nothing,
Become a luminous pearl!
Come down from the heavens,
And live in the ocean.[25]
You are a flashing sword,
Strike terror into the world's soul;
Come out of the scabbard and show your mettle.
Spread an eagle's wings
And spill the pheasants' blood.[26]
For a falcon, living in the nest spells death.[27]
You do not yet know this,
But with union comes the end of longing[28]:
What is eternal life?
To burn – and keep on burning![29]

IV. ADAM SPEAKS ON COMING OUT OF PARADISE

How good it is[30]
To fill life with passion and longing;[31]
In one breath[32] to melt the heart
Of desert, mountain and wild;
To open the door of the cage[33]
On to a spacious garden;
To take the path to the heavens,
And speak with the stars in confidence;
To cast – at times with secret longing,
But with a show of humility at times –
A knowing glance at the sanctum of His Glory;[34]
At times to see
Nothing but The One in throngs of tulips,
But at times to tell
The prickly thorn apart from the rose![35]

My whole being is a flame that burns for ever,[36]
And is full of the pain of desire.[37]
I would exchange certainty for doubt –
For I am dying to know and discover.[38, 39]

V. THE MORN OF RESURRECTION

Adam in the presence of God

You, whose sun gives the star of life its splendour,[40]
With my heart you lit
The candle of the sightless world![41]
My skills have poured an ocean into a strait,[42]
My pickaxe makes milk flow from the heart of stone.[43]
Venus is my captive, the moon worships me;
My reason,[44] which does great deeds,
Subdues and controls the universe.
I have gone down into the earth,
And been up into the heavens,
Both the atom and the radiant sun
Are under the spell of my magic.[45]
Although his[46] sorcery[47] deluded me,
Excuse my fault, forgive my sin:[48]
If his sorcery had not taken me in,
The world could not have been subdued.[49]
Without the halter of humility,
Pride could not be taken prisoner.[50]
To melt this stone statue[51] with my hot sighs,
I had to don his *zunnar*.[52]
Reason catches artful nature in a net –
And thus Ahriman, born of fire,
Bows down before the creature of dust![53]

PM 244-7 [255-8]

[1] *Love . . . blood!* In its encounter with (Divine) Beauty hitherto, Love had fared poorly because it had never had in its ranks anyone bold enough to accept the challenge of Beauty. Love saw a fearless champion in Adam and rejoiced. 'Who would roll his heart in blood' means a true lover, one who is prepared to undergo the trials of love and would not hesitate to lay down his life in the cause of love.

[2]*Beauty . . . born!* For the first time Beauty felt that someone who would size her up had been born. The thought of being exposed to a penetrating gaze made Beauty shudder.

[3]*Nature . . . over himself:* The world, being governed by natural laws, had no independent will, and it was therefore difficult to conceive of, or account for, a being that was born from the materials of such a predetermined world and yet possessed critical self-awareness ('. . . Make and unmake . . . watch over himself'). But one could imagine that, if created, such a being, instead of submitting to the laws of nature, would have a shaping influence on the world. The thrust of the lines is that Adam's birth suggested staggering possibilities of exploiting the resources of the universe. To 'watch over onself' (*khud-nigare*) here simultaneously means (1) 'to guard and preserve oneself' and (2) to 'monitor and assess oneself critically'.

[4]*From the heavens . . . all veils!* In one's sleeping-chamber one is hidden from view. 'Eternity's sleeping-chamber' was the repository of all possibilities that till then had remained unrealised, and so were like secrets kept from view. It was feared that Adam would translate those possibilities into realities and thus reveal those secrets.

[5]*Desire, resting . . . was born:* Adam's birth awakened slumbering ambition and created a new spirit of adventure – in short, it gave an impetus to action.

[6]*Life said . . . ancient dome:* Life up till now had been locked up inside the dome of the universe (the image is of the dome of the sky). With the birth of Adam it saw an 'opening' or a 'window of opportunity' for itself.

[7]*my element is fire:* In Part II, quite appropriately, images of fire – of both heat and light – predominate.

[8]*I am the bond . . . elements:* Iblis claims to control nature at all levels, the highest as well as the lowest.

[9]*burn:* Intransitive verb.

[10]*the alchemist's fire:* The fire used by the alchemist in his workshop to transmute base metal into gold.

[11]*From my . . . rest:* The reading in the Sheikh Ghulam Ali edition – *az zav-i man mawjah-i charkh-i sukun na-pazir* – is followed here rather than that in the Iqbal Academy edition: *az zav-i man mawjah-i charkh sukun na-pazir*. (I have been told that the comma which separates *charkh* from *sukun* in the latter edition is an error and will be deleted in the next printing.)

[12]*existence:* The word in the original – *paykar* – literally means 'form, figure, mould'.

[13]*You rob . . . sloth:* The word used for 'sloth', *sukun*, signifies inertia here. Iblis means that God, like a robber, means to cheat Adam of his glorious destiny by accustoming him to a life of *sukun*. In the original the *ba* in the phrase *tu ba-sukun rahzani* may be taken to denote 'to' or 'towards' rather than 'with' or 'by means of', and the line would then mean: 'You misguide people into slothful behaviour'.

[14]*I guide . . . passion:* Iblis claims that, unlike God, he rouses Adam to action, which is what constitutes true guidance. Here too the *ba* in *man ba-tapish rahbaram* may be taken to mean 'to' or 'towards' (see previous note), the phrase now meaning 'I guide aright to burning passion'. In either case the word *tapish*

would be ironic, since it suggests the heat – or fire – of hell, hell being the punishment for following Iblis.

[15]*I did not . . . me:* The allusion is to God's command to angels to bow down before Adam, although Iblis disparagingly calls that command a supplication. Angels are called 'paupers' because they were 'poor' in self-esteem – they were only too ready to uncritically obey God's command. Iblis considers it beneath himself to receive homage from such gutless beings. Iblis's contempt for the angels is obvious. 'I did not beg . . . ' implies: But God did!

[16]*I am mighty . . . resurrection:* Unlike God, Iblis does not need the instruments of hell and resurrection to obtain submission.

[17]*Adam – that creature . . . arms!* This is both a challenge and a prediction.

[18]*A life . . . quiet:* This is the basic line of argument employed by Iblis: action is better than inaction – and this is claimed to be true in absolute terms.

[19]*Even a dove . . . eagle:* Although they make sense on their own, these lines can be taken as a reply to an unexpressed question. After hearing Iblis's call for action, Adam may have asked (or the question may have arisen in his mind): But how may I start living a life of action?'

[20]*The waters . . . action:* In paradise there are *Kawthar*, a stream, and *Tasnim*, a fountain (Qur'an 108:1 and 83:17, respectively). The meaning is that the sweet and delicious waters of the heavens have turned Adam into a lazy man.

[21]*Take wine . . . grapes:* Muslims are supposed to abstain from wine in this world (Qur'an 5:90-91) but are promised pure wine in the next world (56:17-19; 76:21). Iblis, on the contrary, wants Adam to give up heavenly drinks and enjoy the wine of this world – genuine wine, made from grapes.

[22]*'Good' and 'bad' . . . in action:* Action and movement are self-justifying and do not need the sanction of an outside authority.

[23]*Come . . . kingdom!* An allusion to Qur'an 20:120, where Iblis asks, 'Shall I guide you to . . . a kingdom that will not perish?'

[24]*go about . . . offer:* Iblis is not unlike a salesman who invites a prospective customer to enter a store and look around, confident that the customer will be compelled to buy in the end.

[25]*Now you are . . . ocean:* Departure from heaven will transform Adam, just as (according to a poetic myth) a raindrop, after separating from the clouds, enters a body of water, lives in a shell and, after going through several stages, becomes a pearl.

[26]*Spread . . . blood:* Again, an invitation to action for its own sake, and an appeal to the human beings' 'animal' instinct. 'You are a drop of water of no worth' reminds one of the Qur'anic phrase (22:8; 77:20) *ma' mahin*, 'worthless water' (seminal fluid), a reference to the humble origins of human beings.

[27]*For a falcon . . . death:* Iblis's systematic persuasion of Adam continues. Cf. the opening lines of this part where Iblis exhorts Adam, now timid like a dove, to become a bold eagle.

[28]*But with . . . longing:* After attaining a goal, the seeker loses interest in it. Likewise, being with God for ever will kill the longing for God.

[29]*To burn . . . burning!* Literally 'to burn incompletely' (see the introduction to

this chapter). To burn with desire for something unattainable, to long unceasingly for something that eludes one's grasp – that is true, eternal life!

[30]*How good it is:* Although it is not mentioned, and he probably does not realise this, Adam has swallowed Iblis's bait.

[31]*To fill life . . . longing:* Cf. the opening of Part III. Adam uses the same expression as that used by Iblis – 'passion and longing' (*soz-o-saz*) – to describe the ideal life. See also nn. 33, 36, below.

[32]*In one breath:* The Persian word *dam* ('breath') as used here may have Sufi connotations. Certain breathing techniques used by Sufis during spiritual exercises are supposed to give special powers.

[33]*the cage:* In Part III Iblis described heaven as a 'trap'; Adam's use of 'cage' for heaven shows the extent to which Iblis has been able to influence Adam's thought and vocabulary (see also n. 31, above, and n. 36, below).

[34]*To cast . . . His Glory:* This is a hint that Iblis's plan will crack from within. Human beings, even when they break with their Creator, have an affinity with Him and long to be reunited with Him (Adam, after all, lived in or close to the divine sanctum, which he will always remember with fondness even when he is away from it). Iblis had not reckoned with this.

[35]*At times to see . . . rose!* To see unity in multiplicity and *vice versa* – that is the highest intellectual exercise of which human beings are capable. The human wish to be close to the Creator is again obvious.

[36]*My whole . . . for ever:* Adam seems to have an insatiable urge to know and discover. The original, *hamah soz-i na-tamamam*, means literally 'My whole being is an incomplete burning'; a fire that burns incompletely is one that keeps burning and is never extinguished. This statement also echoes Iblis (see last lines of Part III; see also nn. 31, 33, above). But Iblis's description of eternal life as a state of constant burning may be an ironic pointer to his never-dying hatred of both God and Adam on the one hand, and to his own punishment in hell in the next world on the other. By contrast, Adam's description of his own state as constant burning represents a simple and innocent curiosity on his part to know about the world, as is borne out by the concluding words of this part.

[37]*And is . . . desire:* The pain that results from the failure to satisfy one's wishes, or rather from pursuing a lofty but unattainable ideal.

[38]*I would . . . discover:* These lines have an ominous, Faustian ring. The word for 'committed' in the original is *shahid*, literally 'martyr'. In the present context, *shahid* has the metaphorical sense of one who has an intense desire to do something. But the word here also carries the ironic suggestion that Adam, like Faust, is willing to pay with his life in order to quench his thirst for knowledge and experience that may be beyond the reach of ordinary mortals. Cf. 'The Perfume of the Flower', Chapter 10.

[39]Part IV bears comparison with the concluding part of Milton's *Paradise Lost* where Adam, accompanied by his mate Eve, leaves paradise and first sets eyes on the world. There is, however, a crucial difference: while Milton's Adam is a sad figure, who even inspires pity ('Some natural tears they dropped, but wiped them soon', *Paradise Lost,* Book XII, l. 645), Iqbal's, possessing as he

does an irrepressible spirit of adventure and a deep sense of curiosity, evokes admiration.

[40] *You, whose . . . splendour:* Unlike Iblis, whose address to God begins on a negative note (Part II), Adam makes a 'proper' beginning – by praising Him.

[41] *With my . . . world!* It was through the agency of human beings that God transformed this dark and dismal world into a bright and beautiful place.

[42] *My skills . . . strait:* I have worked wonders and accomplished much. 'My skills have poured an ocean into a strait' brings to mind human accomplishments like the building of the Suez Canal, and it is perhaps not too far-fetched to suggest that Iqbal had this engineering feat in mind here.

[43] *My pickaxe . . . stone:* 'To make milk flow from rock with one's pickaxe' is a Persian (and also Urdu) idiom meaning to perform an extraordinary task. This is an allusion to the remarkable feat performed, according to a Persian legend, by Farhad who used his pickaxe to cut a passage through rocks and allow a stream of milk from mountain pastures to flow through it and reach the pools of his beloved Shirin's castle.

[44] *reason:* As pointed out in the introduction to this chapter, the word in the original – *ᶜaql* – here stands for both reason and the intellect.

[45] *Both . . . magic:* Like Iblis (see Part II), Adam claims to have gained complete mastery over nature. But while he is proud of his achievements, Adam has not become arrogant like Iblis. See also n. 48, below.

[46] *his:* Iblis's. The use of a pronoun to refer to Iblis suggests that he is (at least in the context of this poem) a familiar figure, there being no need to name him. Cf. Chapter 1, 'Whose World is This, Yours or Mine?', n. 4.

[47] *sorcery:* Adam uses the word 'magic' (*jadu*) to describe his own mastery over nature, but 'sorcery' (*fusun*, literally 'enchantment') of Iblis's attempt to mislead him. The two words, as used here, have different connotations: magic is legitimate, whereas sorcery, being illusion and deceit, is forbidden. Using his words with care, Adam seeks to distance himself from Iblis.

[48] *Excuse . . . sin:* Note that while Iblis (Part II) first defied the divine command and then explained why he refused to bow down before Adam, Adam here first seeks God's forgiveness and only then presents his excuse. Such an unconditional apology clearly sets him apart from Iblis, and, one would think, stands a good chance of being accepted.

[49] *If his . . . subdued:* This is the principal basis of Adam's defence. Unlike Iblis, whose refusal to bow down before Adam was the result of overweening pride, Adam says that his deception by Iblis afforded him the opportunity to conquer nature, which in turn led to his defeat of Iblis.

[50] *Without . . . taken prisoner* The strategy (used, for example, in martial arts) of 'yield and you will overcome'.

[51] *stone statue:* The Persian is *but-i sangin*. Both words in this construction are significant. *But* is an idol that is perceived as claiming deity and demanding worship and loyalty, but in romantic parlance the word means 'one of statuesque beauty'. Likewise, *sangin* means 'made of stone', but also 'one [usually a beautiful woman] with a heart of stone'. In describing Iblis as *but-i sangin*, Iqbal plays

on the different meanings of the two words: Iblis has deceptive charm and is a tough opponent. See also n.52, below.

[52] *I had . . . zunnar:* The *zunnar* is the ritual thread worn by high-caste Hindus. Adam says that it was necessary for him to wear Iblis's *zunnar,* i.e. to become his devotee, in order to get close to him and bring him under control.

[53] *And thus . . . dust!* Only in this way could the divine command have been carried out – the command given to Iblis, who is made of fire, to bow down before Adam, who is made of earth. In Zoroastrianism, Ahriman is the principle of darkness or evil, Ahura Mazda being the principle of light or good. Adam equates Iblis, who is made of fire, with Ahriman. This is significant because Zoroastrianism, to which Ahriman belongs, is based on fire-worship, fire being considered good and holy. Iqbal's verse thus suggests that Iblis-as-Ahriman has falsely set himself up as the god of fire, and must be subdued.

3

SATAN'S VIEWPOINT

Iqbal was fascinated by the figure of Satan, and in several poems discussed and analysed his personality and his role in the existential framework. For Iqbal, Satan (or Iblis – his Qur'anic name) is not merely evil incarnate but has a full-blown, complex personality that calls for close and even, in a certain sense, sympathetic study. The two poems in this chapter illustrate some of the intriguing aspects of this figure as found in Iqbal's poetry.

The Fall of Adam was preceded by another fall – that of Iblis, whose refusal to obey the divine command to bow down before Adam led to his expulsion from the heavens (Qur'an 7:13, 18; 15:34; 38:77). According to the Qur'an, while Adam repented and was forgiven, Iblis persisted in his refusal, thus incurring God's eternal wrath. In the first poem, 'Gabriel and Iblis', Iqbal interprets the Fall of Iblis, offering what may be called a psychological explanation of it from Iblis's point of view.

Gabriel and Iblis, who had been friends in the celestial spheres, happen to meet long after Iblis's Fall. Gabriel opens the conversation by asking how Iblis is, and Iblis describes briefly but pungently the agony he is in. But as the conversation progresses, with Gabriel asking Iblis whether the latter may still mend his ways and thus be able to re-enter the heavens, Iblis begins to fill with pride as he recalls how momentous his defiance of God proved to be: his act changed the fate of Adam and set off, on earth, the struggle between good and evil. Thanks to his defiance, the world is full of activity and excitement, in contrast to the heavenly spheres where dead silence prevails. By the end of the poem Iblis has succeeded, mainly through auto-suggestion, in putting a bold face on his suffering: the satisfaction of being a rival to God fills him with sufficient pride to justify his act of defiance, an act which caused him the pain to which he refers at the start of the poem. So, by invoking his pride to numb his pain, Iblis further incriminates himself – again in contrast to Adam who, on reflection, repented and was forgiven by God. But while one sees that Iblis is stubborn in his refusal to submit to God, it is impossible not to note a certain tragic streak in his character as drawn by Iqbal: for all his bravado, Iblis betrays clear signs of an inner anguish which he may succeed in suppressing for a while, but which he will perhaps never get rid of completely. Iblis's auto-suggestion not only proves therapeutic, as just noted; it also helps to transform him from an introvert to an extrovert. When Gabriel opens the conversation by asking Iblis a question, Iblis is taciturn and gives a one-line answer, but on being probed further he offers a more detailed answer, in which he analyses his own situation. He begins by recognising the gravity of his crime, but ends on a note of self-justification. By now he has developed a high degree of self-confidence. When Gabriel makes his next comment, Iblis answers him in even greater detail, using aggressive language. The change in Iblis's attitude and speech is gradual but unmistakable.

'Give Me Another Adversary!' is a highly satirical poem. Iblis, the speaker, is less than gratified that he has been able to walk all over Adam (or human beings), and requests God to give him a stronger adversary, one who would 'wring' his neck. Adam was supposed to defeat Iblis but has become his willing victim, to the extent that Iblis disdains to have him as his rival. This is the ultimate disgrace for Adam – or for humanity. The poem is thus really about human moral failure. As for Iblis, he comes across as a being who, with all his faults, possesses a certain moral courage, which seems to be the only virtue he claims. Whether or not Iblis is actually justified in claiming it is a question to which Iqbal typically avoids giving an answer.

GABRIEL AND IBLIS

GABRIEL

Old friend, how goes the world of colour and smell?[1]

IBLIS

Burning and suffering, scars and pain, seeking and longing![2]

GABRIEL

They are all talking about you in the celestial spheres.
Could your ripped garment still be mended?[3]

IBLIS

Ah, Gabriel, you do not know this secret:
When my wine-jug broke it turned my head.[4]
I can never walk this place again![5]
How quiet this region is! There are no houses, no streets![6]
One whose despair warms the heart of the universe –
What suits him best, 'Give up hope!' or 'Don't give up hope!'?[7]

GABRIEL

You gave up exalted positions when you said 'No'.[8]
The angels lost face with God – what a disgrace that was![9]

IBLIS

With my boldness I make this handful of dust rise up.[10]
My mischief weaves the garment that reason wears.[11]
From the shore you watch the clash of good and evil.
Which of us suffers the buffets of the storms – you or I?[12]
Both Khizr and Ilyas feel helpless:[13]
The storms I have stirred up rage in oceans, rivers, and streams.
If you are ever alone with God, ask Him:
Whose blood coloured the story of Adam?[14]

I rankle in God's heart like a thorn. But what about you?
All you do is chant 'He is God!' over and over![15]

BJ 473-4 [435-6]

[1]*the world of colour and smell:* The terrestrial world, to which Iblis was banished. In the present context the phrase used in the original, *jahan-i rang-o-bu,* may contain one or all of the following suggestions: (1) Gabriel is unwittingly contrasting the colourful life on earth with the rather bland heavenly life; (2) he acknowledges that Iblis, though expelled from the heavens, has been able to turn the earth into a fine, attractive place; (3) he is being mildly satirical: it is this world of *false* colour and *deceptive* smell that was to be Iblis's lot.

[2]*Burning . . . longing!* Iblis acknowledges the unhappy consequences of his defiance of God: life after his exile from the heavens has been full of suffering.

[3]*Could . . . mended?* 'To mend one's ripped garment' is a metaphor for making amends or reparation (cf. the English 'to patch up'). Gabriel is suggesting that Iblis should repent and seek God's forgiveness.

[4]*When . . . head:* Iblis cites wounded pride as the cause of his defiance. The wine-jug stands for pride and the broken jug for Iblis's wounded pride; and having one's head turned stands for the reckless act of defying God resulting from wounded pride. The expression *sar-mast* in the original carries three interrelated meanings: (1) drunk or inebriated, (2) rash or reckless (as when one's head has been turned), and (3) conceited.

[5]*I can . . . again!* Iblis realises, perhaps more fully than Gabriel, the gravity of his crime. What makes Iblis a tragic figure is that he not only has pride but is also painfully aware – and perhaps has been from the very beginning – of the consequences of the act of defiance which pride led him to commit.

[6]*How quiet . . . streets!* This line represents a dramatic turning-point in the poem. As he talks to Gabriel, Iblis suddenly becomes conscious of the complete and unrelieved silence of the heavenly region. He finds this unsettling, for by now he has become used to the excitement of earthly existence. That excitement comes from Iblis himself, as he will soon remark. He feels that not only is it impossible for him to return to the heavens but he would not like to do so even if it were possible. There are no signs of life and activity in the heavens – no houses or streets – and this deadness makes them desolate and uninviting

[7]*One whose . . . 'Do not give up hope!'?* The moment he becomes conscious of the contrast between the heavenly and terrestrial regions, Iblis thinks of how he contributed to transforming the earth into a remarkable place. True, he has despaired of ever re-entering the heavens, but then it is to his despair that the world ultimately owes its charm and beauty. Qur'an 39:53 says that one should not despair of God's mercy, for He has the power to forgive all one's sins. Iblis, however, would prefer despair to hope, because his despair has been creative and fruitful.

[8]*You gave up . . . 'No':* You forfeited the exalted position you had in the eyes of God, and also the position to which you would have risen if you had obeyed Him.

[9]*The angels . . . was!* Gabriel here reminds Iblis of the collective responsibility

of the angels to maintain an unblemished image; Iblis violated this principle of collective responsibility. In his response, which follows, Iblis ridicules the idea.

[10] *With my . . . rise up:* Iblis claims to have taught human beings ambition, and so would like to get credit for their accomplishments. The line is suggestive in another sense. In the Qur'an (see 7:12; 38:76), Iblis justifies his refusal to obey God by saying that a creature of fire would not bow down before a creature of dust; this implies that fire, whose natural tendency is to rise, is superior to earth, whose natural tendency is to drop to the ground and lie there. So with evident pride Iblis says in this line that the element of earth (Adam or humanity) has learnt from the element of fire (Iblis) how to rise, grow and develop, that the would-be recipient of homage from Iblis is beholden to him and ought therefore to pay him homage.

[11] *My mischief . . . wears:* The resourcefulness of reason is due to me, and without my mischief, which impels and invigorates it, reason would not be the creative force it is.

[12] *Which . . . I?* To Iblis, Gabriel is a mere spectator of the struggle between good and evil, whereas Iblis is part of it. Although he made the wrong choice at the beginning and has suffered because of it, Iblis in his own mind considers himself a cut above Gabriel, a non-participant observer of the struggle. The basic premise of Iblis's argument is that action, even when evil, is preferable to inaction.

[13] *Both . . . helpless:* Khizr (also Khizar; Arabic Khidr) is the name tradition and legend have given to the unnamed person in the Qur'an (18:65-82) appointed by God to initiate Moses into some of the divine mysteries. Khizr is believed to possess special powers and is represented as the guide and rescuer of those who have lost their way, whether on land or at sea. The name of Ilyas (Elijah of Tishbe of the Bible) is also associated with supernatural powers (see 1 Kings 17-18); he is said to have risen to heaven alive in a whirlwind (2 Kings 2:11). Iblis says that even persons with supernatural powers cannot come to the rescue of those overtaken by the storms he raises. See also Chapter 10, 'The Duck and the Crocodile', n. 1.

[14] *If you are . . . Adam?* A subtle suggestion that even God acknowledges the 'contribution' Iblis has made to the drama of history. There is a further suggestion that while God would not acknowledge this in front of ordinary angels, He might do so if an angel of Gabriel's rank were to ask Him – privately. In other words, God would make the admission only if the matter is kept off the record. Iblis here puts himself on a par with God – at Gabriel's expense: only God and Iblis appreciate the true significance of Iblis's act of defiance; Gabriel has no idea of it.

[15] *I rankle . . . over and over!* Iblis is a rival of God Himself, which God recognises –to His discomfort. As for Gabriel, he is merely engaged in meaningless repetition of the hymnic formula, 'He is God!'

GIVE ME ANOTHER ADVERSARY!

Lord of Right and Wrong,[1]
I have been corrupted by Adam's company![2]
Not once did he shake his head at my command;[3]
He has shut his eyes to his own self,
And has failed to discover who he is.
The earth he is made of is not inclined to rebel –
There is no spark of pride in him.[4]
The quarry says to the hunter, 'Catch me!'
I beg to be spared from such a willing slave!
Spare me from such quarry –
Remember my faithful service to You in the past![5]
He has weakened that noble resolve of mine.[6]
O misery!
He has a base mind and a feeble will;
This rival of mine cannot withstand one of my blows.
I deserve a man with a penetrating look,[7]
A truly seasoned rival.
Take back this toy of water and clay –
Old men cannot act like children![8]
The son of Adam is only a handful of straw!
And for that one spark of mine is enough.[9]
If straw is all that this world had,
Why was I given so much fire?
To melt glass is a disgrace;
To melt stone – that is a true feat!
My victories have forced my back up against the wall,[10]
So that I have come to seek restitution from You.
I want from You one who will truly deny me[11] –
Give me one like that,
Lead me to such a man of God.
He should be one who would wring my neck,
Whose very look will cause me to quake,
A man who will say, 'Get out of my sight!',
And in whose eyes I will not be worth two grains of barley.

A living man, God, who lives truth!
In defeat, perhaps, I will find pleasure.

JN 609-10 [725-6]

[1]*Lord . . . Wrong:* There is – possibly deliberate – ambiguity here: is Iblis simply stating what he believes to be an objective fact, namely that God alone determines and is therefore the sole source of ethical value, or is he implying blame, even with satirical intent, by suggesting that God is the author not only of good but also of evil?

[2]*I have . . . company!* By 'Adam' Iblis means not only the first human being created by God, but also humankind in general. And so he is simultaneously insinuating that in the Garden of Eden it was Adam who led him astray and not the other way round, and that his statement is based on his experience with countless human beings on earth over a very long period of time.

[3]*Not once . . . command:* The standard by which Adam is judged here and found wanting is supplied by Iblis himself, who questioned the wisdom behind God's command to him to bow down before Adam.

[4]*There . . . him:* This is Iblis's main criticism: Adam is too servile and does not know how to assert his independence and be his own master. But while Iblis's diagnosis may be correct, the cure he suggests for Adam is typically Satanic: like Iblis, he must become rebellious. As can be seen, Iblis's prescription consists of only one ingredient – pride – or what the Greeks called *hubris*. 'The earth he is made of is not inclined to rebel' is true in a literal sense also: earth obeys the law of gravity whereas fire seems to defy it (see n. 10 to previous poem). So from Iblis's point of view, Adam's physical constitution (biology, as some would say) is his destiny.

[5]*Remember . . . past!* Deliver me from such quarry in the name of my past service to you. It is said that Iblis was a great worshipper of God before he disobeyed Him.

[6]*He has . . . mine:* The demonstrative 'that' in the Persian phrase (*past az'u an himmat-i wala-i man*) is significant: with obvious pride Iblis refers to his previous defiance of the divine command to bow down before Adam. Note that defiance of God rather than obedience to Him is set up as a positive value (cf. n. 11, below).

[7]*a man with a penetrating look:* The phrase *sahib-nazar* in the original implies simultaneously (1) one who is intelligent (so that he will not easily be fooled by Iblis); (2) one who can see through others (so that he will size up Iblis); and (3) one whose mere glance brings about instantaneous spiritual transformation in others (this last meaning is Sufic and would suggest, if obliquely, that even Iblis has a secret desire to undergo transformation at the hands of an accomplished spiritual master – if such a person can be found).

[8]*Take back . . . children!* The words 'water and clay' represent children's play (one can picture children playing in a sandbox with a bucket of water). The line means that Iblis is too advanced in years to be entertained or diverted like a child. But the phrase 'water and clay' also stands for Adam or human beings, for the Qur'an says that God made every living thing from water (21:30), and

that Adam and human beings were made from earth (e.g., 3:59 and 18:37), the two statements taken together again amounting to 'water and clay' (see also 37:11, which says that God made human beings from *tin lazib*, 'sticky clay'). Iblis would thus be saying that he is too seasoned and sophisticated to have Adam or his progeny as his playmates, for, compared with him, they are like children. The words 'take back' (*baz gir*) in this case become significant: in the beginning Iblis was quite willing to accept the challenge of fighting a moral duel with Adam, whom he had willingly 'received' from God. But experience convinced him that Adam could be beaten too easily, and this realisation caused disappointment to the self-respecting Iblis, who now wants God to 'take back' this creature of water and clay. Iblis is like a customer who eagerly buys something in a store but, on inspecting it later, is dissatisfied and wishes to return it.

[9] *And for . . . enough:* Note the consistent use of the fire image by Iblis in this poem – fire being the constitutive element of Iblis himself; he has already used the phrase 'spark of pride', and will soon refer to the melting of glass and stone.

[10] *My victories . . . wall:* A pun may be intended in the original. *Futuhat* ('victories') literally means 'openings' (a victory 'opens up' a land for the victor), but in Iblis's case they have actually had a 'straitening' effect, the phrase *tang amadan* being the equivalent of 'to be driven into a corner, to be pushed to the wall, to be left with few options'.

[11] *one who will truly deny me: Munkir* means 'one who denies, repudiates, refuses to accept'. It is an Islamic term signifying one who rejects the truths one ought to accept. Iblis appropriates the term, standing it on its head (cf. n. 6, above).

4
THE HUMAN CONDITION

As a reflective person, Iqbal was acutely aware of the painful aspects of human existence. In his poetry he notes, analyses and comments on these aspects. For all its buoyant optimism, his poetry is permeated by a certain sadness, which however is not without a certain dignity and even grandeur. The poems of this chapter represent Iqbal's thoughts on the unique but paradoxical situation of human beings in the universe.

The first poem, 'Man', contrasts human with natural existence. Nature is in a state of complete peace with itself, since the phenomena of nature are content with their situation: they willingly submit to a set of laws laid down for them, and have no desire to question their fate – or discover the meaning of existence. But the human mind seeks answers to questions it finds disturbing. The irony, however, is that human beings have been made seekers of secrets which have been hidden from them. The irony is doubled when one realises that the contrast between human and natural existence is not merely theoretical. Human beings do not live in isolation from nature but in the midst of it. Thus their loneliness is not that of one sulking in private, but is such as can exist in the midst of a revelling crowd: a merry, carefree nature seems to mock the troubles of humankind.

The second poem, as its title suggests, deals with the same theme of human solitude, but from a different angle. One way of stating the difference between the two poems 'Man' and 'Solitude' is that the first is marked by reflection and the second by action. In 'Man' the poet is in a pensive mood and does nothing about his solitude. In 'Solitude' he is past the stage of reflection and vigorously enquires why he has been placed in his particular situation. This poem explores the meaning and significance of human existence, but the result of the exploration is not stated there may even be a suggestion that such exploration is futile. Nothing can be said with certainty about the poem's final message, although several possibilities suggest themselves. Conscious of possessing a feeling heart, the poet (who represents humanity) contrasts himself with the universe. In succession he approaches the sea, the mountain and the moon, asking each whether, like him, it possesses a heart. All are embarrassed at the question and remain silent, for none of them has a heart. Finally the poet arrives in the presence of God and complains that he has no companion in the vast world God has created: nothing in the universe possesses a heart, whereas he, although a handful of dust, is all heart. At this God smiles, but He too remains silent.

What are we to make of all this? It is obvious that the universe, despite its gigantic proportions and impressive phenomena, lacks that priceless thing called heart – which is possessed by human beings and which makes them superior to the universe. The French thinker Pascal said that human greatness consists in the consciousness human beings have of their weakness: 'Man knows that he is wretched. He is therefore wretched, because he is so; but is really great because he knows it'. And 'Man is but a reed, the weakest in nature, but a thinking reed'. Consciousness, then, is the distinctive feature of human existence and more than makes up for human physical weakness or inferiority. In the poem 'The Moon' in *Bang-i Dara* (105-6 [78-80]) Iqbal compares himself with the moon and notes a few similarities, but then says:

And yet, O shining moon,
We are so different from each other!
The heart that feels pain
Is a different heart indeed.
Though I am all darkness and you are all light,
Yet you are far removed from the station of awareness.
I know the purpose of my life –
And this is a radiance your face does not have.

Thus, at one level 'Solitude' argues for the superiority of human beings to the universe. But the important question is why does God smile in silence? There are several possible explanations:

1. Possession of a feeling heart distinguishes the poet (again, a representative of humanity) from the rest of creation and sets him

above it. But this secret was hidden from the poet, not in order to keep him ignorant of his distinction but in order to motivate him to discover it through his own effort. Discovery of the secret earns him praise from God: he has risen to his Creator's expectations, and the Creator smiles in appreciation.

2. The discovery is painful. The poet's search for a 'heart' in nature was caused by his desire to find a companion with whom he could converse and share his joys and sorrows. But nature can offer him no solace, and the search, which makes him aware of his distinctive position in the universe (see last paragraph), also leaves him high and dry. God smiles in compassion, even pity.

3. The discovery, though painful, is not without meaning. For if the poet has failed to find a companion, then at least he can be a companion to himself. Put differently, instead of turning to lifeless, or rather heartless, nature in search of companionship, he should cement his bonds with the rest of the human race. The painful discovery will thus redirect the poet's attention towards humanity, and God smiles not so much at the poet's present failure to find a companion in nature, but at the possibilities that lie hidden in the discovery, which he will soon make, of how strong are the bonds of humanity.

4. The poet is about to discover that God Himself is the friend he needs – and deserves. The divine smile signals the discovery.

5. If God is the friend the poet needs and deserves, then this may be true not simply because no one else is fit to be his companion, but also because, like the poet, God too is alone. If indeed this is true, then God smiles because He too is happy – at finding a companion in the poet.

None of these interpretations finds conclusive support in the poem. Is the ambiguity deliberate? Possibly Iqbal does not want to provide a neat solution to a complex problem.

The sequence of the poet's queries is notable. He first approaches the sea, then the mountain which is at a higher altitude, then the moon which is at a higher altitude still, and finally God who is in the highest heavens. At each level the problem, one senses, becomes more acute.

The third poem, 'The Dew and the Stars', presents a bleak picture of the human situation. To talk about the world of human beings is to tell an endless tale of woe. This world, which has the aspect of a pretty garden, is actually filled with sorrow and pain, and the beautiful things in it perish all too quickly. The moon foolishly hopes that the earth will heal its 'scar,' and so revolves around it like a lover (see n. 11). The conclusion drawn by the dew is that the world is no more than 'A picture of lament drawn on the canvas of space'.

The last poem, 'The Story of Adam', has an undercurrent of sadness, but ends on a more hopeful note than 'The Dew and the Stars'. It is an account of the extraordinary diversity of the human career on earth. The human being has played the roles of prophet and reformer, idolator and iconoclast, poet and thinker, martyr and killer, recluse and warrior, explorer and adventurer. But there is one thing that runs through this chequered career like a constant: awareness. This came about as a result of Adam drinking the 'cup of awareness' in Eden. The wine he drank made him forget his covenant with God, and, banished to a 'foreign land' (earth), he roamed from place to place, assuming a variety of roles. The search for the truth about things led to his making remarkable discoveries, but it also caused him to make mistakes. The secret of existence remained elusive until it dawned on him that it was to be found not in the external world – which by then he had reduced to subjection – but inside himself. The distinction of human beings is thus to be explained in terms of what is their unique possession: the heart (cf. 'Solitude' in this chapter).

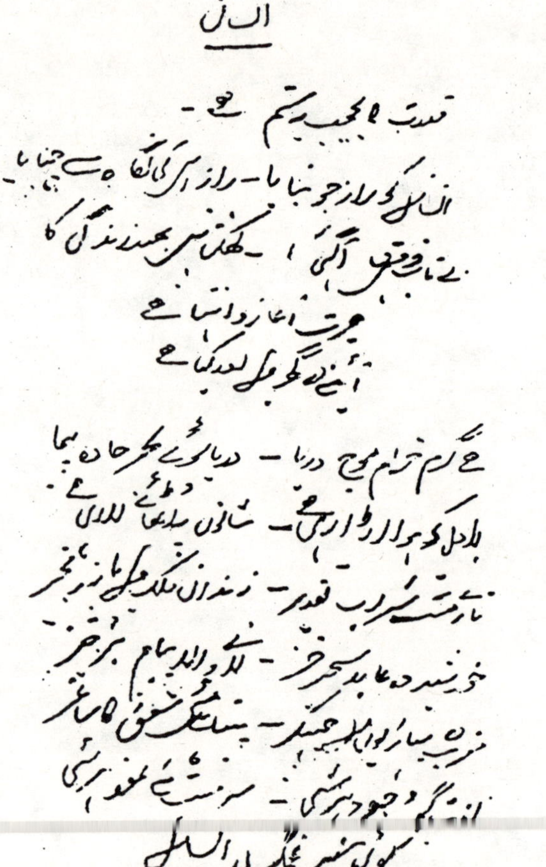
انسان

قدرت کا عجیب یہ ستم ہے

انساں کو راز جو بنایا — راز اس کی نگاہ سے چھپایا

بے تاب ہے ذوق آگہی کا — کھلتا نہیں بھید زندگی کا

حیرت آغاز و انتہا ہے

آئینے کے گھر میں اور کیا ہے

ہے گرم خرام موج دریا — دریا سوئے بحر جادہ پیما

بادل کو ہوا اڑا رہی ہے — شانوں پہ اٹھائے لا رہی ہے

تارے مست شراب تقدیر — زندان فلک میں پا بہ زنجیر

خورشید وہ عابد سحر خیز — لانے والا پیام برخیز

مغرب کی پہاڑیوں میں چھپ کر — پیتا ہے مے شفق کا ساغر

لذت گیر وجود ہر شے — سرمست مے نمود ہر شے

کوئی نہیں غمگسار انساں

کیا تلخ ہے روزگار انساں

Ms. of Poem 'Man' (in Urdu)

MAN

Nature has played a strange and wanton joke –
Making man a seeker of secrets,
But hiding the secrets from his view!
The urge for knowledge gives him no rest,
But the secret of life remains undiscovered.
Wonder is at the beginning and the end –
What else is there in this house of mirrors?[1]
The wave of the river glides along,
The river follows its course to the ocean,
The wind sweeps the clouds along,
Bearing them on its shoulders,
The stars are drunk with the wine of fate,[2]
And lie chained in the sky's prison;
The sun, a worshipper who gets up at dawn,
And calls out the message 'Arise!',
Is hiding in the western hills,
Drinking a cup of reddish wine.[3]
All things delight in their very existence,
They are drunk with the wine of being.[4]
But there is no one to drive away his sorrow –
How bitter are the days of man!

BD 152-3 [126-7]

[1] *Wonder . . . mirrors?* A 'house of mirrors' is one made of mirror glass or one full of mirrors. A mirror, if a surprised person looks in it, will reflect and thus compound the surprise. The world is called a house of mirrors here because it reflects and compounds the surprise one feels on account of the undiscovered secrets and unsolved mysteries of existence it contains. And this surprise grows through every moment of life, so that wonder is 'at the beginning and the end'.

[2] *The stars . . . fate:* The stars passively obey the laws decreed for them.

[3] *The sun . . . reddish wine:* The sun is first likened to a devout believer who rises at dawn to perform the prayer (first of the five obligatory daily prayers in Islam, performed shortly before dawn), and then to someone who likes to get drunk in the evening. Since Islam forbids the drinking of wine (Qur'an 5:90-91), the contrast between the sun's worshipfulness and drunkenness here suggests – playfully, of course – hypocrisy (note also that the sun drinks while hidden from view, being 'ashamed' of doing what is forbidden). In the poem the sun drinks red wine, similar to the colour of the sky at sunset. Its roundness is likened to

that of the wine-cup. In Persian, one phrase for the sun's disk is *jam-i malik-i sharq*, literally 'the wine-cup of the king of the east'.

[4]*They are . . . being:* All things relish the fact of having emerged from the void and now having existence. Manifestation of the self (*khudi*) is one of the major themes of Iqbal's poetry (see Chapter 12, section '*Khudi*'), and according to Iqbal all things seek self-expression.

SOLITUDE

I went down to the sea,
And said to the restless wave,
'You are for ever searching – what is your trouble?
Your bag[1] contains a thousand glowing pearls –
But do you, like me, have in your breast
A pearl of a heart?'
It writhed in pain and drew away from the shore –
It did not say a word.

I went up to the mountain and said,
'How unfeeling you are!
Have the sighs and screams of a soul in torment
Ever reached your ears? If within your rocks
There is only one diamond formed from a drop of blood,[2]
Then come for a moment
And talk to a wretched man like me'.[3]
It withdrew into itself and held its breath –
It did not say a word.

I travelled far, and asked the moon,
'Your lot is to keep travelling,
Is it also your lot to reach a destination?[4]
Your face sends out rays
That turn the world into a land of jasmine.[5]
But does the radiance of the scar on your face
Come from the glow of a heart or not?'[6]
It cast a jealous glance[7] at the star[8] –
It did not say a word.

I left the moon and the sun behind,
And reached the presence of God.
I said, 'Not one atom in Your world
Is intimate with me.
The world has no heart,
But I, though a handful of dust, am all heart.
It[9] is a pleasant garden, but unworthy of my song!'[10]

A smile appeared on His lips –
He did not say a word.

PM 272–3 [288]

[1]*bag:* The word in the original is *giriban,* literally the 'opening at the breast of a garment'.

[2]*If within . . . blood:* If you possess a heart.

[3]*a wretched man like me:* Wretched because, possessed of a heart, the poet observes and feels the pain and misery found in the world.

[4]*Is it . . . destination?* The implication, of course, is that the moon is denied a destination or a resting-place. In the poem 'The Thoughts of Stars' in *Payam-i Mashriq* (253 [265]), one star says to another:

> We are in the midst of an ocean, no shore is in sight:
> It is our fate to travel on,
> But this caravan has no destination.

[5]*Your face . . . jasmine:* Your rays shed brightness on the world, so that white jasmine appears to be blooming all around.

[6]*But does . . . heart or not?* Is the scar you bear on your face – and even this scar is bright! – due to the inner glow of a heart you might possess or is it due to a borrowed fire?

[7]*jealous glance:* The word *raqibanah* in the original means literally 'like a rival'. See also next note.

[8]*the star:* The word 'star' may be generic, in which case it would mean 'stars', implying that the light of the stars is original to them, whereas the light of the moon is borrowed. But the word may refer specifically to the sun, from which the moon borrows its light. This would be appropriate since the poet later mentions both the moon and the sun ('I left the moon and the sun behind . . .').

[9]*It:* The world or universe.

[10]*unworthy of my song!* This is because the poet's song arises from his heart and a heart is needed to appreciate it, whereas the universe has no heart.

THE DEW AND THE STARS

One night the stars said to the dew:
'Every morning you get to see new sights.
Who knows how many worlds you have seen!
You have seen the traces left behind by those
Who once flourished but then perished.[1]
Venus has heard this news from an angel:
Far, far from the heavens is the city of men.
Tell us the story of that beautiful realm
Which is serenaded by the moon.'[2]

'Do not ask me, stars, about the garden of the world;
It is no garden, but a town filled with sighs and screams.
The west wind arrives there, only to leave again;
The poor bud blooms, but only to wither.
How do I describe to you
The bud that brightens the garden –
It is a tiny flame with no heat![3]
The rose cannot hear the nightingale's cry,
Or pick up pearls from the fold of my hem.[4]
The songbirds are captive – what an outrage![5]
Thorns grow in the rose's shadow – what an outrage![6]
The eyes of the ailing narcissus are never dry.[7]
The heart longs to see, but the eyes are blind.[8]
The ardour of its complaint has burnt the tall tree's heart;
The tree is a captive, and is free only in name.[9]
The stars – in the language of men – are sparks struck by
human sighs;[10]
In the language of gardens, I am the sky's tears.
It is foolish how the moon circles the earth –
It believes that the earth will heal the scar in its heart![11]
The world is a cottage built in the air –
A picture of lament drawn on the canvas of space.'

BD 244-5 [215-6]

[1] *You have . . . perished:* You know the history of nations which rose to prominence but were then wiped out of existence.

[2]*Which . . . moon:* The moon revolves around the earth, singing it love-songs.

[3]*It is . . . heat!* Just as a flame without heat cannot make fire, so the bud of this worldly garden will not become a flower – if it does, it will remain one in name only, lacking the attributes of a true flower.

[4]*Or pick . . . hem:* The rose is so firmly rooted in the ground that it cannot collect the pearls which the dew has brought in its folded hem. Here dew-drops are likened to pearls.

[5]*The songbirds . . . outrage!* It is a shame that the birds which fill the air with melody are put behind bars for singing. In other words, merit and quality remain unrewarded. It is implied that the incompetent and undeserving (the birds with ugly voices) are esteemed and glorified.

[6]*Thorns . . . outrage!* The beautiful things of this world are left to the mercy of evil forces.

[7]*The eyes . . . dry.* In Persian and Urdu poetry the languid eyes of the female beloved are often likened to the narcissus, their peculiar look suggesting infirmity and thus imparting to the beloved a charming languor of movement. Here the narcissus itself is pictured as ailing, with its eyes moist from tears, but the reason given for its ailment is its sorrow at the suffering in the world.

[8]*The heart . . . blind:* There is an unbridgeable gap between human ambition and human ability. This thought frequently occurs in Iqbal's poetry (e.g. the poems 'Listen to Me!' in Chapter 1 and 'Man' earlier in the present chapter).

[9]*The ardour . . . name:* In Persian and Urdu poetry, trees that are tall and erect are often pictured as walking or strolling. Possibly this is because one of the charming attributes of the female beloved was her erect stature. At first a pretty woman was likened to a tall, upright tree like the cypress or pine, and then by transference her gait was attributed to the tree itself. With motion having become a normal attribute of the tree, its immobility was now considered abnormal. This is the point made here: the tall tree (*shamshad*) of the garden complains that it has been chained to the ground, whereas it should have been free to move. Tragically, the ardour with which it complained has consumed its heart.

[10]*The stars . . . sighs:* The sighs heaved by luckless human beings had such fervour that they produced sparks, which rose to the skies and were named stars.

[11]*the scar in its heart!* In Urdu poetry, the man in the moon becomes the scar of the moon's heart. In the context of this poem (cf. last poem, n. 6, and 'Prayer' in Chapter 11, n. 10) the scar is something the moon wishes to be rid of.

THE STORY OF ADAM

What a story I have to tell, to anyone who will listen,
Of how I travelled in foreign lands![1]
I forgot the story of the First Covenant.[2]
In the garden of heaven,
When I drank the fiery cup of awareness I felt uneasy.[3]
I have always searched for the truth about the world,
Showing the celestial heights of my thought.[4]
Such was my fickle temperament
That in no place under the sky could I settle for good.
At times I cleared the Kaᶜbah of stone idols,[5]
But at times put statues in the same sanctuary;[6]
At times, to savour talk, I went to Mount Sinai,[7]
And hid the eternal light in the folds of my sleeve;[8]
By my own people I was hung on the cross;[9]
I travelled to the skies, leaving earth behind.[10]
For years I hid in the Cave of Hira;[11]
I served the world its last cup of wine;[12]
Arriving in India, I sang the Divine Song;[13]
I took a fancy to the land of Greece;[14]
When India did not heed my call,
I went to live in China and Japan;[15]
I saw the world composed of atoms,
Contrary to what the men of faith taught.[16]
By stirring up the conflict between reason and faith,
I soaked in blood hundreds of lands.[17]
When I failed to probe the reality of the stars,
I spent nights on end wrapped in thought.[18]
The sword of the Church could not frighten me;[19]
I taught the proposition of the revolving earth.[20]
I donned the lens of far-seeing reason,
and told the world the secret of gravity.[21]
I captured rays[22] and the restless lightning,[23]
Making this earth the envy of paradise.
But although my reason held the world captive to my ring,
Yet I remained ignorant of the secret of existence.[24]

When at last my eyes, worshippers of appearance, were opened,
I found it already lodged in the mansion of my heart![25]

BD 108-9 [81-2]

[1]*foreign lands!* Paradise was Adam's real home, so that the earth, to which he was banished after committing the sin of eating the forbidden fruit, was foreign territory (*ghurbat*) to him. The speaker is evidently nostalgic.

[2]*I forgot . . . Covenant:* According to Qur'an 7:172, God in pre-existence brought forth the progeny of human beings from their loins and asked them whether they recognised Him as their Lord. All replied in the affirmative. This was the First Covenant, since it preceded all others.

[3]*In the garden . . . uneasy:* The awareness resulting from eating the forbidden fruit led to Adam's dissatisfaction with life in paradise. The wine is called 'fiery' in the sense that it stirred Adam's soul, causing him to behave recklessly. *Jam-i atishin*, the Persian phrase used in the original for the 'fiery cup' (of awareness), also alludes to Satan or Iblis, whose constitutive element is fire, and who in fact was responsible for misleading Adam, causing him to drink the 'wine'.

[4]*Showing . . . thought:* Demonstrating, in my search, the remarkable human capacity for thought and reflection.

[5]*At times . . . idols:* Muhammad purged the Ka^{c}bah of statues.

[6]*But at times . . . sanctuary:* In pre-Islamic times the Arabs had put statues in the Ka^{c}bah.

[7]*At times, to savour . . . Sinai:* A reference to Moses who spoke with God (Qur'an 4:164). The word used in the text for 'Sinai' is *Tur* (in the Qur'an the mountain is called *Tur Sayna'* [23:20] and *Tur Sinin* [95:2]). 'To savour talk' means 'to have the pleasure of conversing with God'.

[8]*And hid . . . sleeve:* One of the miracles which God gave to Moses to use against Pharaoh was that of the white hand: Moses drew his hand in to his side, and when he brought it out it had become shining white (Qur'an 27:12; 28:32). 'To have something up one's sleeve' is an idiom in Urdu as well as in English. The Urdu expression as used here is, however, different from the English in two ways: it combines the literal and metaphorical meanings, and it does not have the negative sense of cunning, although it does suggest that Moses, in his confrontation with Pharaoh, had a surprise in store for him. The 'light of eternity' (*nur-i azal*) would ordinarily mean the light of God's being – for God is light (see Qur'an 24:35) – and this light must be conceived of as having existed since eternity. But the phrase may refer to the whiteness of Moses' hand – and because it was God who had given that miracle to Moses, it could by extension be called the light of eternity. The use of the phrase seems deliberately ambiguous.

[9]*By my . . . cross:* This is a reference to Jesus (although it may be interpreted in more general terms), and is an example of how a writer, especially a poet, may appropriate for literary or aesthetic purposes a tenet, image or idea that is peculiar to another tradition but is viewed differently in the writer's own (Islam does not accept the view that Jesus was crucified [see Qur'an 4:157]).

[10]*I travelled . . . behind:* According to the Qur'an, Jesus was raised to the heavens (Qur'an 4:158), and in the Bible (2 Kings 2:11) the prophet Elijah of Tishbe (called Ilyas in the Qur'an) entered heaven in a whirlwind. Although a reference to Muhammad's ascension is not ruled out, the words 'leaving earth behind' (more literally 'abandoning earth' [*chhor kar zamin*]) seem to apply primarily to Jesus and Elijah.

[11]*For years . . . Hira:* Before becoming a prophet, Muhammad used to go to the Cave of Hira (Arabic: Hira') for meditation; he received his first revelation there.

[12]*I served . . . wine:* Muhammad, who is regarded as the Last Prophet (Qur'an 33:43 calls him the 'Seal of the Prophets'), communicated the last message from God to humankind.

[13]*the Divine Song:* The Hindu religious classic *Bhagavad Gita.*

[14]*I took . . . Greece:* A reference to the era of the great thinkers of ancient Greece.

[15]*When India . . . Japan:* A reference to the rise of Buddhism in protest against Hindu Brahmanism and its spread in lands outside India.

[16]*I saw . . . taught:* The view that the world is composed of atoms and that its movements can be explained in natural and mechanistic terms without reference to a supernatural being is attributed to the pre-Socratic Leucippus and Democritus, especially the latter, and to the post-Aristotelian Epicurus, who accepted a modified version of it. The view, whose classic exposition is to be found in the Latin poet Lucretius' *The Nature of Things*, is predicated on materialistic assumptions and explains away spirituality (even the soul is said to be composed of atoms). As such it would obviously be unacceptable to the advocates of religion.

[17]*By stirring . . . lands:* The conflict between faith and reason in history has been both bloody and long-drawn-out.

[18]*When I . . . thought:* A reference to the dedicated work of astronomers in different eras of human history.

[19]*The sword . . . me:* A reference to such figures as the Italian philosopher Giordano Bruno, who refused to retract statements which the Church found heretical and was consequently burnt at the stake (1600), and the Italian astronomer and physicist Galileo (1564-1642), who faced the Inquisition for holding heretical views.

[20]*I taught . . . earth:* Copernicus (1473-1543) taught that the earth rotates on its axis and revolves around the sun.

[21]*I donned . . . gravity:* Isaac Newton (1642-1727) discovered the law of gravity. Note the wordplay in the poem. 'The lens of far-seeing reason' is, in the original text, *ayinah-i ᶜaql-i dur-bin*. The last word in the phrase, *dur-bin*, when used of a human being, means 'farsighted'. But it also means 'telescope' and *ᶜaql-i dur-bin* may therefore mean either 'farsighted reason' or 'telescope-equipped reason'. Newton, of course, discovered the law of gravity by using his 'farsighted reason' which, it is here implied, was as powerful as the eye equipped with a telescope.

[22]*I captured rays:* The reference is to the X-ray, discovered by the German physicist Wilhelm Conrad Röntgen (1845-1923).

[23] *the restless lightning:* The English scientist Michael Faraday (1791-1867), inventor of the first dynamo, 'harnessed' lightning – or electricity.

[24] *But although . . . existence:* I remained unaware that none of these otherwise impressive discoveries and inventions would provide a clue to the particular secret of human existence (see the concluding lines of the poem). The phrase 'captive to my ring' alludes to King Solomon who is said to have controlled the *jinn* (genies) with the power of his magic ring.

[25] *When at last . . . heart!* The main obstacle to my being able to fathom the secret of existence consisted of my own eyes, which were concentrated on the apparent and the phenomenal, whereas the secret of existence had all the time been locked away in my own heart, and all I had to do was look inside it.

5

HEAD AND HEART

In several poems Iqbal explores the relation between reason and intuition, intellect and emotion, knowledge and love – or, in simple terms, between head and heart. His use of several pairs of correlatives to describe the relation between the two indicates that Iqbal regards it as complex. He recognises that head and heart are often in conflict, although each has its particular merits. In the first poem in this chapter, reason and heart both assert their claims to pre-eminence. Reason opens the conversation and claims to be the rescuer and guide of the lost, dismissing the heart as a mere drop of blood. In its reply the heart acknowledges the merits of reason, but draws attention to its own superior powers; while reason perceives the outward aspect of things, the heart has access to the inmost recesses of reality; reason guides one to truth, but truth without beauty is stark and lustreless. Furthermore, reason must work within the framework of space and time, whereas the heart does not labour under any such restrictions. The heart closes its speech by calling itself the throne of God.

From this poem we see that Iqbal does not belittle reason, although he believes that it has certain inherent limitations. Reason, to its credit, enables one to analyse matters, provides solutions to the ordinary, day-to-day problems of life, and proves a sure guide in organising life in general. But it controls the external life of human beings. It perceives whatever has form, but the spirit or essence of things often eludes it. It illuminates the dark alleys of existence, but the light it provides has no warmth. Only feeling, intuition or love embodied in – or rather symbolised by – the heart imparts to life depth or verticality and imbues it with true worth and quality.

The second poem, also in dialogue form, takes the discussion a step further, for here there is an attempt to resolve the conflict between head and heart. Knowledge boasts that it is aware of the secrets of the heavens and the earth and rules the world.

There follow a eulogy of knowledge gained from sensory sources ('An eye that I am . . .') and a contemptuous dismissal of knowledge that deals with heavenly or spiritual matters. Knowledge, we are told, is something to be made public – something 'to be brought to the market place' – and not kept hidden. This is a pre-emptive criticism of love, which would keep rather than divulge secrets. In its response love first points out the 'mischief' knowledge has caused in the world (from the lines that follow we gather that this is caused by knowledge uninformed by love, such knowledge being called an illusion, magic trick or sorcery). But then love remarks that knowledge, too, is holy in origin and was meant to be in harmony with love and not in opposition to it. Love and knowledge are like twins, so they should be allies and not rivals.

Iqbal's final view, then, is that there should be complementarity rather than opposition between knowledge and love – or head and heart. But it is obvious that he accords a higher status to the heart. In both poems the heart's position is stated in greater detail and more forcefully. The head in both poems (that is, reason in the first, knowledge in the second) comes across as self-centred, even arrogant, and sneers at its interlocutor. The heart, on the other hand, while not denying the powers of the head, still asserts its own superiority, and does so cogently. In the second poem, the heart (love) invites the head (knowledge) to reunite with it, for this would enable knowledge to transform the world into a paradise. This last comment may be taken as representing Iqbal's view that while knowledge divorced from love is a force of destruction, knowledge informed by love becomes a great constructive force for human society.

REASON AND HEART

One day reason said to the heart:
'I am a guide for those who are lost.
I live on earth, but I roam the skies –
Just see the vastness of my reach.
My task in the world is to guide and lead,
I am like Khizr of blessed steps.[1]
I interpret the book of life,
And through me Divine Glory shines forth.
You are no more than a drop of blood,
While I am the envy of the priceless pearl!'

The heart listened, and then said:
'This is all true,
But now look at me,
And see what I am.
You penetrate the secret of existence,
But I see it with my eyes.
You deal with the outward aspect of things,
I know what lies within.[2]
Knowledge comes from you, gnosis from me;[3]
You seek God, I reveal Him.
Attaining the ultimate in knowledge only makes one restless –
I am the cure for that malady.[4]
You are the candle of the Assembly of Truth;
I am the lamp of the Assembly of Beauty.[5]
You are hobbled by space and time,[6]
While I am the bird in the Lotus Tree.[7]
My status is so high –
I am the throne of the God of Majesty!'[8]

BD 72-3 [41-2]

[1] *I am like . . . steps:* On Khizr see Chapter 3, 'Gabriel and Iblis', n. 13. He is called one 'of blessed steps' because (1) the ground where he sets his foot is said to turn green (cf. the Persian saying *Khizr bahar dar qadam darad*, 'Spring comes in the wake of Khizr'), and (2) his arrival on a scene augurs well – he guides those who have lost their way and rescues those in distress. Reason thus claims to be a deliverer from doubt or uncertainty.

[2] *You deal . . . within:* The outward pertains to the phenomenal world, the inward to matters of the heart and soul.

[3] *Knowledge . . . me:* The words used for 'knowledge' and 'gnosis' are *ʿilm* and *maʿrifat* (Arabic *maʿrifah*) respectively. In Muslim mysticism a distinction is often made between *ʿilm* and *maʿrifah*, the former representing bookish (and, as such, shallow and imperfect) learning, the latter intuitive (and, as such, profound and authentic) knowledge.

[4] *Attaining . . . malady:* 'The height of knowledge is bewilderment' is a familiar Islamic saying, signifying that the path of knowledge ultimately brings one to a point where one is lost in wonder, and more questions stare one in the face than those to which one has found answers. In other words, knowledge or intellectualism, instead of bringing contentment, breeds discontent and restlessness. In Islamic history the example of the theologian-mystic Ghazali (d. 1111) is often cited to show that ultimate satisfaction is to be found in spirituality rather than in intellectualism.

[5] *You are . . . Beauty:* Reason is concerned with *identifying* truth and falsehood, the heart, with *appreciating* beauty. The lines can be interpreted mystically, truth and beauty representing, respectively, Divine Truth and Divine Beauty. The meaning in this case would be that reason, using the means of discursive analysis at its disposal, can arrive at a cognitive understanding of the Truth, but love alone has the power – by intuition – to experience the Divinity's attribute of Beauty. Cf. 'Shakespeare' (Chapter 7), where Iqbal calls beauty the 'mirror of truth'.

[6] *You are hobbled . . . time:* You are limited by space and time, which are necessary to your operation. Space and time, as Immanuel Kant says in a different context (see Chapter 7, introduction), are the essential prerequisites of experience.

[7] *I am the bird . . . Tree:* In my freedom from the limitations of space and time I am like a bird perching in the Lotus Tree. The word used for the 'Lotus Tree' is *sidrah*, which points to the fuller, Qur'anic name of the tree, *Sidrat al-Muntaha* (literally the 'lotus tree of the boundary' – the 'boundary' suggesting the farthest point in the celestial regions accessible to human beings), by which, according to Qur'an 53:13-14, the Prophet Muhammad, during his ascension to the heavens, saw Gabriel. Association with the heavens, Gabriel, and Muhammad thus enables the heart to claim holiness for itself. The heart's claim to be a bird of the Lotus Tree becomes significant when compared with reason's boast (made at the beginning of the poem) that it can fly as high as the skies. The heart says that, for all its power of flight, reason remains confined to the four corners of the physical universe, whereas the heart has access to the highest celestial regions.

[8] *I am the throne . . . Majesty!* According to a Sufi or popular saying, the world is too small a place to house God, but the believer's heart is large enough to house Him.

A DIALOGUE BETWEEN KNOWLEDGE AND LOVE

KNOWLEDGE

My eyes have witnessed
The secrets of the seven and the four,[1]
And with my lasso I have captured the world.
I am an eye, and when I was opened I turned this way –
Why should I bother about the other side of the heavens?[2]
A hundred songs flow from my instrument;
I bring to market every secret I know.[3]

LOVE

Because of the spell you have cast the sea is in flames,
The air spews fire and is filled with poison.[4]
When you and I were friends, you were a light;
But you broke with me, and your light became a fire.[5]
You were born in the innermost sanctum of the Divinity,
But then fell into Satan's trap.[6]
Come – turn this earthly world into a garden,
And make the old world young again.[7]
Come – take just a little[8] of my heart's solicitude,
And build, under the heavens, an everlasting paradise.[9]
We have been on intimate terms since the day of creation,
And are the high and low notes of the same song.[10]

PM 254–5 [267–8]

[1]*The secrets . . . four:* The seven heavens and the four directions, that is, the whole universe.

[2]*I am . . . heavens?* i.e. praise of sensory knowledge and dismissal of spiritual knowledge as baseless or irrelevant.

[3]*I bring . . . know:* I publicise what I know and do not conceal it. The phrase 'I bring to the market place' (*ba-bazar afganam*) suggests honesty and transparency: I reveal fully.

[4]*Because of . . . poison:* Most of your accomplishments are illusory, and are also destructive in character.

[5]*When you and I . . . fire:* Knowledge becomes destructive when it breaks off its relation with its twin, love, because it then becomes callous.

[6]*You were . . . trap:* You are holy in origin, but you fell victim to Satan. Iqbal

may be alluding to the story of Adam and Satan, in which case he would be suggesting that Adam's Fall was the result of a failure of love on Adam's part.
[7]*And make . . . again:* Love keeps the world young. Separated from love, knowledge turns into a force of destruction, and in consequence the world starts to 'age'.
[8]*just a little:* Literally 'an atom' (*yak dharrah*).
[9]*Come – take . . . paradise:* Knowledge can transform the world into a paradise only when it begins to 'feel' for the world. Even a small amount of love's solicitude for the welfare of the world would enable knowledge to do marvels.
[10]*We have been . . . song:* We are two complimentary beats of the same rhythm.

6
THE POET

In more than one place Iqbal says that he does not wish to be admired or remembered as a poet. For possibly the greatest poet of the Indian subcontinent in the twentieth century to say that may appear strange, but it is more easily understood if we remember that in Iqbal's time 'poetry' often implied the art of composing verses whose distinguishing features were affected sentiment, contrived elegance and shallowness of thought. Because Iqbal meant to use poetry to communicate a fairly coherent set of ideas on certain subjects, he could have little sympathy with the view of art for art's sake, especially in a backward and decadent society. The poet, in his view, had a mission to perform, and its nature is explained in several poems.

In the first poem in this chapter Iqbal calls the poet the eye of the nation. The metaphor brings to mind three roles of the poet: those of guide (like the eye, the poet looks out, guiding the nation on its path), visionary (like a seer, he has insight into the future and wishes to share this with others), and well-wisher or comforter (he is full of sympathy for the other members of society, and, like the eye, weeps at their sufferings). One of the main functions of the poet, in Iqbal's view, is to serve as society's conscience.

In the second poem, 'The Night and the Poet', the night asks the poet why he alone is awake while all the rest of the world is asleep. The poet replies that he has a message of love to deliver but his people are either unprepared or unwilling to receive it. Wishing to share it with somebody, the poet tells the message to the stars of the sky. The poet's despondency is the result of his failure to find a receptive human ear, and it is implied that nature sometimes provides better companionship than human beings are capable of.

In the third poem, 'The Houri and the Poet' (which, as the Urdu subtitle indicates, was written in response to Goethe's poem

'Dichter und Huri'), the houri asks the poet why he is uninterested in the pleasures of paradise. The poet, being an idealist, replies that paradise, which represents perfection, cannot satisfy him because he is always in search of something more perfect, a possibility that is excluded in paradise. Paradise is all happiness and joy, and there is no room in it for sorrow and pain. Iqbal is not advocating masochism. The pain and sorrow of love are felt because of the realisation that one's lofty ideals will be for ever unattainable. The capacity to feel pain and sorrow in this sense gives the highest pleasure – what Iqbal calls at the beginning of the poem the pleasure afforded by the sharp thorn. If 'The Houri and the Poet' is read together with other poems such as 'The Night and the Poet', the love Iqbal speaks of may be identified as love of one's community or, more generally, love of humankind.

THE NATION'S EYE

A nation is like a body,
And the individuals in it the body's limbs:
Those who walk the road of industry
Are its hands and feet,
The office of government is its beautiful face,
And the poet of tuneful melodies is its seeing eye.[1]
If just one limb should suffer pain,
Tears will drop from the eye –
How anxious the eye is for the whole body!

BD 93 [61]

[1]*seeing eye: Didah-i bina,* the phrase in the original signifies both sight and insight.

THE NIGHT AND THE POET

THE NIGHT

Why do you roam about in my moonlight,
So worried,[1]
Silent as a flower, drifting[2] like perfume?
Perhaps you are a jeweller
Dealing in the pearls that are called stars,
Or are a fish that swims in my river of light;
Or a star that has fallen from my brow,
And, having forsaken the heights,
Now resides in the depths below.
The strings of the violin of life are still;
My mirror reflects life as it sleeps.
The eye of the vortex too is sleeping
In the depths of the river;
The restless wave hugs the shore and is still.
The earth, so busy and bustling,
Slumbers as though no one lived on it.
But the poet's heart is never at peace –
How did you elude my spell?

THE POET

I sow pearls in the soil of your moon;
Hiding from men, I weep like dawn.[3]
I am reluctant to come out in the busy day,
And my tears flow in the solitude of night.
The cry pent up inside me,
Whom should I get to hear it,
And to whom can I show my burning desire?
Lying on my chest the lightning of Sinai[4] sobs:
Where is the seeing eye – has it gone to sleep?[5]
My assembly-hall[6] is dead like the candle at a grave.[7]
Alas, night! I have a long way to go!
The winds of the present age are not favourable to it[8]:
It does not feel the loss it has suffered.

The message of love,
When I can no longer keep it to myself,
I come and tell it to your shining stars.

BD 200-1 [172-3]

[1]*worried:* The Persian word used is *parishan.* For the play on this word, see n. 2, below.

[2]*drifting:* The word in the original is, again, *parishan,* which means both 'worried' (cf. n. 1, above) and 'scattered' (the second meaning is intended in this line). Iqbal thus plays on the word, using it twice in the opening lines, once in each sense.

[3]*I weep like dawn:* I shed tears, which are like dew-drops – the tears shed by dawn, which is lonely like me.

[4]*the lightning of Sinai:* The Persian phrase *barq-i ayman* means literally either 'the blessed lightning' or 'the lightning that shone on the right side [of Mount Sinai]', but in either case makes reference to the experience of Moses on Sinai as related in the Qur'an. The phrase represents a confluence of two Qur'anic descriptions: (1) The part of Mount Sinai where Moses was addressed by God and given the Law is called in the Qur'an *janib at-tur al-ayman* (the blessed [*or* right] side of the mountain – 19:52); see also 20:80 where the construction translates as 'the blessed side of the mountain' and 28:30. (2) When Moses expressed his wish to see God, God manifested Himself on Mount Sinai, or rather on a part of it, which was crushed to pieces under the impact of the divine epiphany, Moses himself falling down unconscious (*sa*ʿ*iqa*; 7:143). From the second description Iqbal borrows the word *barq* (this word does not actually occur in 7:143, although it is clearly suggested by the words *tajalla* and *sa*ʿ*iqa*), and from the first description *ayman,* and coins the phrase *barq-i ayman.*

[5]*Lying on my . . . sleep?* The lightning is likened to a grieving child who clings to his parent, seeking comfort or relief. Unlike the *barq-i ayman* of Moses (see last note), which brought life to the Israelites, the *barq-i ayman* of Iqbal generates no enthusiasm in the audience: there are no eyes to notice it! This causes grief to the lightning itself. The image is a bold one, for it suggests that Iqbal's message is comparable to that of Moses. Note also the oxymoron in 'The lightning of Sinai sobs' – it is as if a fire were shedding tears.

[6]*assembly-hall: Mahfil,* the word in the original, means both (1) a gathering-place and (2) people who have gathered in a place. Iqbal is referring to the Muslim community, which seems to be without life or spirit, for it does not respond to his message.

[7]*like the candle at a grave:* That is, like the candles which people light at the graves where the bodies are newly buried and which burn out after some time.

[8]*it:* The 'assembly-hall', or the people gathered there – again, the Muslim community.

THE HOURI AND THE POET

THE HOURI

You are not attracted to wine,
And you do not look at me:
How surprising that you do not know
The art of mixing!
It is but a tune of quest, a flame of desire,
Your sigh, your song.[1]
With your song you have made
Such a lovely world
That paradise itself appears to me
To be some conjurer's trick.[2]

THE POET

You charm travellers' hearts with pointed talk,[3]
Except that, in the pleasure it gives,
One cannot compare it with the sharp thorn.[4]
What can I do, for by nature I am not someone
Who can live for long in one place!
My heart is restless,
Like the west wind in a field of tulips.
The moment my eyes light upon a pretty face,
My heart begins to long for one prettier still.
In the spark I seek a star, in the star a sun:
I have no wish for a destination,
For if I stop I die.
When I get up, having drunk
A cup of wine matured by one spring,
I begin to sing another verse,
And long for yet another spring.
I seek the end of what has no end –
With a restless eye, and hope in my heart.
The lover's heart dies in an eternal heaven –
In it no afflicted soul cries,
There is no sorrow, and no one to drive sorrow away![5]

PM 279-80 [296-8]

[1]*How surprising . . . your song:* The houri is surprised to note that the poet – even though he has reached paradise, the most perfect of all places and one that is the ultimate goal of all mortals – is uninterested in the pleasures available to him and is still searching for something else

[2]*With your song . . . trick:* Even paradise appears to lack reality and substance in comparison with the beautiful world you have created by means of your songs.

[3]*You charm . . . talk:* The Persian phrase used for pointed talk is *kalam-i nesh-dare*, (see n. 4, below). The word 'travellers' proleptically suggests that, for the poet at least, paradise is not the final destination. The line possibly alludes to the sirens of Greek mythology.

[4]*Except that . . . thorn:* The Persian used for 'sharp thorn' is *nok-i khare*. The *nok* (point) of the thorn is thus compared with the *nesh* (literally 'lancet') of the houri's talk, referred to in the opening line of the poet's response. See introduction to this chapter, and next note.

[5]*In it no . . . away!* The pangs of love a lover feels give him a special pleasure, which he cannot experience in the otherwise perfect paradise. In an eternal paradise, therefore, the lover's heart will wither and die.

7
PERSONALITIES

Iqbal wrote poems about many distinguished figures of national, regional and world history. He comments on their work and contribution, noting their distinction, recording his admiration for them, and acknowledging, explicitly or implicitly, his intellectual or spiritual debt to them. I have chosen only a few of these personalities, but the selection reflects not only the range of Iqbal's scholarship but also the broad humanity of his sympathies.

The first poem in this chapter is about Abu Bakr, the most famous Companion of the Prophet Muhammad and the first caliph of Islam after the Prophet. Abu Bakr's deep commitment to Islam and unswerving devotion to the Prophet earned him from the latter the nickname *Siddiq* (the truthful), which is the title of the Urdu poem. That certain other Companions of the Prophet should compete with Abu Bakr for distinction was only natural. One such was ʿUmar, who later succeeded Abu Bakr as caliph. On a certain occasion the Prophet called upon the affluent Muslims to spend their wealth in the way of God. ʿUmar, seeing this as an opportunity to outmatch Abu Bakr, brought half of all his wealth and handed it over to the Prophet – but he could not win the contest. Iqbal offers a moving poetic version of the historical incident.

Nanak (*c.* 1469–*c.* 1539) is considered the founder of the Sikh religion in India. Sikhism, which represents a revolt against Hindu idolatry, was influenced by the monotheistic teachings of Islam. In 'Nanak' Iqbal first laments the fact that India, in the end, proved inhospitable to Buddhism (founded in the 6th and 5th centuries BCE), which was a reaction against the oppressive Brahmin rule in the country; Buddhism finally prospered outside India. Most of the poem appears to be about the resistance India offered to Buddhist ideas, with Nanak being mentioned only in the last few lines. On reading the poem carefully one realises, however, that the mention of Buddhism only serves to introduce, in a dramatic way, Nanak and his monotheistic message. For all her stupor and imperviousness, India could not ignore Nanak's powerful voice. Unlike Buddhism, which had to leave India, Sikhism fought for a place, and succeeded in establishing itself, in India.

In the next poem Iqbal compares Shakespeare to the mirror of the human heart – and mind, we might add. Of particular interest in the poem is Iqbal's observation on the remarkable detachment or objectivity Shakespeare was able to maintain in his work – what Keats called his 'negative capability'.

'Rumi and Goethe' – the title of the Urdu poem translates as 'Jalal and Goethe', Jalal being Jalaluddin Rumi (1207-73), the Sufi poet known for his long Persian poem *Mathnawi* – is really about Goethe (1749-1832). Rumi was Iqbal's ideal poet-thinker, and through him he expresses his own admiration for Goethe's *Faust*.

In 'Locke, Kant and Bergson' – the Urdu title is 'Hukama' (Philosophers) – Iqbal summarises some of the essential views of three Western thinkers, writing one couplet about each. The English thinker John Locke (1632-1704) denied the existence of innate ideas, claiming that the human mind at birth is like a 'white paper' with nothing on it. Knowledge, he says, arises from one's experience of the sensory world, sensation thus being the basis of all experience. He accepts reflection as a source of knowledge, but maintains that reflection, too, takes sensory images as its data. The German philosopher Immanuel Kant (1724-1804), while accepting the view of Locke and other empiricists that sensation is the only source of ideas, insists that certain laws are *a priori* basic to all experience. Space (the principle of extension) and time (the principle of motion) supply these prerequisites for experience. Kant also believes that space and time do not give us knowledge of reality as it is (experience of the 'things-in-themselves' always eluding us) but only of the phenomenal aspect of reality. Their differences notwithstanding, Locke the empiricist and Kant the idealist both took a discursive approach to reality, and this is what the French thinker Henri Bergson (1859-1935) finds objectionable. Analysis as a mode of knowing presupposes a static, frozen reality, and in dealing with reality in this form intelligence deals with snapshots of reality rather than with reality itself, which is living, dynamic and indivisible. There is thus a world of difference between reality experienced whole and immediately and reality observed piecemeal and 'mediately'. It is through intuition and not intelligence that one experiences and comes into contact with reality.

Sándor Petöfi (1823-49), the subject of the last piece, was, as the subtitle of the Persian poem explains, a Hungarian poet-soldier who died in a national uprising in his country against Austrian domination. His dead body could not be found, which leads Iqbal to make a highly apposite comment in the last line. Petöfi's poem 'Rise, Magyar' became Hungary's national anthem.

ABU BAKR THE TRUTHFUL

One day the Holy Prophet said to his Companions,
'The rich among you should give in the way of God'.
On hearing that command, an overjoyed ʿUmar stood up;
That day he had thousands of *dirhams*.[1]
Today, for sure, he said in his heart,
My horse will take the lead from Abu Bakr's.[2]
So he brought his wealth to the Trustworthy Prophet[3] –
Sacrifice is needed to start a project off.
'ʿUmar', asked the Prophet, the Sovereign of the world,
'A passion for truth is the sole comfort of your heart.[4]
Did you keep anything back for your family? –
For a Muslim must honour the duty he bears to his relations.'
'Half', he said, 'belongs to wife and children,
The rest I offer to the Community of Light.'[5]

In the meantime that Companion of the Prophet arrived
Who gives strength to the edifice of love and devotion.
No man more loyal, he brought with him
Everything with value in the eyes of the world:
Slaves, money, goods and chattels.
He brought his horses, their hooves shining like the moon,
And his camels, mules and asses.
The Prophet said, 'It is necessary to think of one's family too!'
That man, who knew the secrets of love, said,
'You are the one from whom the moon and stars
Receive the brightness of their eyes;
And you are the one for whose sake
The universe was brought into being:
The lamp is enough for the moth,
The flower is enough for the nightingale –
For Abu Bakr the Prophet of God is enough'.

BD 252-3 [224-5]

[1] *dirhams:* A *dirham* (from the Greek *drachma)* was a silver coin.
[2] *My horse . . . Abu Bakr's:* Today I will outmatch Abu Bakr.

[3]*the Trustworthy Prophet:* A sobriquet (*rasul-i amin* in the original) for the Prophet Muhammad.

[4]*A passion . . . heart:* You are a devotee of truth.

[5]*the Community of Light:* The Muslim community, so called because it walks in or is guided by the light of truth. The expression in the original, *millat-i bayda* (literally 'a community on a clear path') derives from a saying of the Prophet Muhammad.

NANAK

The nation[1] could not care less about Gautama's message –
It did not know the price of its unique pearl![2]
Poor wretches! They never heard the voice of truth:
A tree does not know how sweet its fruit is.
What he revealed was the secret of existence,
But India was proud of its fancies;
It was not an assembly-hall[3] to be lit up by the lamp of truth;
The rain of mercy fell, but the land was barren.
Alas, for the *shudra*[4] India is a house of sorrow,
This land is blind to the sufferings of man.
The Brahmin is still drunk with the wine of pride,
In the assembly-halls of foreigners burns Gautama's lamp.
But, ages later, the house of idols[5] was lit up again –
Azar's house was lit up by Abraham![6]
Again from the Punjab[7] the call of monotheism arose:
A perfect man roused India from slumber.

BD 269 [239]

[1]*The nation:* India.

[2]*unique pearl:* Gautama Buddha.

[3]*assembly-hall:* The word used in the original is *mahfil,* on which see Chapter 6, 'The Night and the Poet', n. 6.

[4]*the shudra:* The low-caste Hindu.

[5]*the house of idols:* Polytheistic India.

[6]*Azar's house . . . Abraham!* According to the Qur'an (6:74), Azar was Abraham's father. He was an idolator, but in his house Abraham, the monotheist, was born. Likewise, the idolatrous land of India was the birthplace of the monotheist Nanak.

[7]*the Punjab:* Nanak arose in the Punjab, one of the provinces of India, now divided into West Punjab (in Pakistan) and East Punjab (in India). Since Partition in 1947, East Punjab has had the largest concentration of Sikhs. The principal Sikh sanctuary is at Amritsar, a city in that province.

SHAKESPEARE

The flowing river[1] mirrors the red glow of dawn,
The quiet of the evening mirrors the evening song,
The rose-leaf mirrors spring's beautiful cheek;
The chamber of the cup mirrors the beauty of the wine;[2]
Beauty mirrors Truth, the heart mirrors Beauty;
The beauty of your speech mirrors the heart of man.
Life finds perfection in your sky-soaring thought.
Was your luminous nature the goal of existence?
When the eye wished to see you, and looked,
It saw the sun hidden in its own brilliance.[3]
You were hidden from the eyes of the world,
But with your own eyes you saw the world exposed and bare.
Nature guards its secrets so jealously –
It will never again create one who knows so many secrets.

BD 279-80 [251]

[1]*The flowing river:* Literally 'the flow of the river'.

[2]*The chamber . . . wine:* The wine is likened to a pretty woman holding a mirror that reflects her beauty – the cup being that mirror. The word used for 'chamber' is *hajlah,* which suggests a bridal chamber, and thus goes well with that image.

[3]*When the eye . . . brilliance:* This image becomes an argument in the statement that follows: one cannot fix one's gaze on the sun because of the brilliant intensity of the rays surrounding it, but the sun itself, being the 'eye' of the heavens, can see the whole world. See the introduction to this chapter for comment on Shakespeare's 'negative capability'.

RUMI AND GOETHE

In paradise that perceptive[1] German
Happened upon the Master of the East.[2]
Where is a poet of such stature! –
Though not a prophet, he is possessed of scripture![3]
To the one who knew divine secrets[4]
He read about the pact of Iblis and the doctor.[5]
Rumi said, 'You who bring words to life,
And hunt angels – and God –
Your thought has made its home
In the inner recesses of the heart,[6]
And created this old world anew.[7]
At one and the same time in the body's frame,
You have seen the tranquillity and the restlessness of the soul,[8]
You have been a witness to the birth of the pearl in the shell.
Not everyone knows the secret of love;
Or is fit to reach these portals.[9]
'He who is blest, and a confidant, knows
That cunning comes from Iblis and love from Adam'.[10]

PM 332 [376-7]

[1]*perceptive:* Literally 'one who understands subtleties' (*nuktah-dan*).

[2]*the Master of the East: Pir-i ᶜAjam* translates literally 'the Master of ᶜAjam', ᶜAjam being Persia or, more loosely, areas other than Arab lands; 'East' seems appropriate in this context.

[3]*Though . . . scripture!* This statement, made by the mystic poet Jami about Rumi and his *Mathnawi*, is here applied by Iqbal to Goethe and his *Faust.* In his *Stray Reflections* (ed. Javid Iqbal; Lahore: Iqbal Academy, 1961; rev. and enlarged edn 1992, p. 74) Iqbal says that *Faust* is 'nothing short of Divine workmanship'.

[4]*the one . . . secrets:* Rumi, admired by Iqbal for his deep insights.

[5]*the pact . . . doctor:* The agreement that the learned Faust would enjoy life to the full for so many years, after which Iblis (Satan) would take possession of his soul.

[6]*Your thought . . . heart:* Your thought has penetrated deep into the hearts of people.

[7]*And created . . . anew:* That is, by retelling, in a graphic manner, the old story of Adam and Satan.

[8]*You have seen . . . soul:* You have seen what gives the soul comfort and what makes it restless during the period of its residence in the body.

[9]*portals:* Portals of love.

[10]*'He who . . . Adam':* A quote from Rumi. The last line means that, for all his failings, Adam is superior to Iblis because, unlike the latter, he retains a certain innocence – born of his love of God (cf. the last section of 'Conquest of Nature' in Chapter 2). In the context of this poem, the remark would mean that Faust, even though he suffered defeat at the hands of Iblis, triumphed over the latter in a certain sense. The word used for 'cunning' is *ziraki*, literally 'intelligence, cleverness, ingenuity'.

LOCKE, KANT AND BERGSON

LOCKE

It was dawn that lit up the tulip's cup
With a drink from the sun;
For the tulip itself bore an empty cup
When it joined the company of flowers.[1]

KANT

By nature it had a taste
For wine that is like crystal:
It is from eternity's sleeping-chamber
That it brings its shining, star-like cup.[2]

BERGSON

It did not bring either wine
Or a cup from eternity:
The tulip gets its eternal passion
From the scar in its own heart.[3,4]

PM 334-5 [381]

[1] A brief explanation of the verse is in order. On entering the world (= when the tulip joins the company of flowers), the human mind is empty (= the tulip's cup is empty). Only when it is exposed to sensory experience (= when it is illuminated by the sun's rays through the agency of dawn) does the mind receive impressions (= that the tulip's cup is filled with wine). In other words, the mind is at first a *tabula rasa*, the source of one's ideas being external. The similarity between Locke's well-known phrase 'empty cabinet' and the 'empty cup' in this verse is obvious and inescapable (see also n. 4, below).

[2] 'It' in lines 1 and 4 stands for the tulip. The wine is 'crystal' in the twin senses of 'clear' and 'bright'. Note that while Locke stresses the original 'emptiness' of the human mind, Kant, although he affirms this emptiness in principle, underscores the importance of the mind as an agent that gives form to experience. Thus the Kantian *a priori* principles, while not creative of experience, are yet necessary to all experience. In its very act of perception, in other words, the mind 'illuminates' the data, which otherwise would have remained in the dark – hence the phrase 'star of a cup'. To sum up, the human mind, even though initially like a clean slate, has an innate capacity for shaping experience. In Iqbal this translates into the following: the tulip, even though it has no wine in its cup, does have a taste for wine. Moreover, since the formative powers of the

mind exist before any experience, Iqbal speaks of the tulip's having brought its shining cup from the sleeping-chamber of eternity (so called because it is the repository of possibilities or potentialities which remain hidden like secrets before being actualised in historical time). See also n. 4, below.

[3]According to Bergson, the real question is not whether the mind is initially blank (Locke) or whether the *a priori* principles give form to sensory data (Kant). Both Locke (the tulip came in with an empty cup) and Kant (the tulip's cup gives shape to the wine that is poured into it) are off the mark. The whole debate between the empiricists and the idealists is irrelevant, for both groups ignore what really matters; in their eagerness to 'understand' reality, they have failed to 'live' reality. Life is not something to be analysed through the use of sophisticated techniques – which is tantamount to dissecting a butterfly. Rather, it should be experienced – intuitively – in all its richness, multiplicity and vibrancy, keeping its integrity uncompromised by the 'machinations' of intelligence. In Iqbal's words, what really matters is that the tulip possesses an abiding passion – the flame of life – whose source lies inside it. The first part of Iqbal's verse about Bergson thus criticises the terms of the empiricist-idealist debate. The second states the essence of Bergson's philosophy: it is the inner quality of life, its impulse to create, and its constant movement that should command one's primary attention. Since it is the inner quality of life that has true value, direct intuition and not intermediary intelligence would be the appropriate means of gaining access to the heart of reality.

[4]A few general remarks on 'Locke, Kant and Bergson' may not be out of place. (1) Iqbal's three couplets are remarkable for their succinct summing up of some of the fundamental ideas of the three philosophers. But Iqbal does not merely state the three philosophers' views; he also shows how these views are interrelated in a continuing movement of thought from Locke to Bergson: how Kant criticised Locke, and how Bergson criticised both Kant and Locke. (2) It is equally remarkable that Iqbal is able to use a single image, that of the tulip, to describe the philosophies of the three thinkers. The tulip, Iqbal's favourite flower, appears ideal for his purposes here: with Locke it becomes a clean slate (empty wine-cup); with Kant it becomes the formal conditioning factors of knowledge and understanding (tulip's starlike cup); and with Bergson the 'scar' in the tulip's heart represents the principle of life which is its own explanation. Iqbal succeeds eminently in explicating certain concepts in Western thought by using a typical Eastern image; one could hardly think of a more felicitous way of describing Western thought to an Eastern audience. (3) To which of the three views is Iqbal himself sympathetic? One can say that, in the present context at least, Iqbal supports the view of Bergson, or that he uses Bergson as his mouthpiece. Bergson would be quite pleased by Iqbal's description elsewhere (*ZK* 638 [589]) of the natural water fountain: 'It is from its inner drive that the water of the fountain gushes forth and rises [*buland josh-i darun se hu'a he fauwara*].'

PETÖFI

In this garden, for just one moment,
You sang of the bride-like rose,
You increased the sorrow of some hearts,
And dispelled the sorrow of others.
You painted the tulip's palm with your blood;[1]
And opened the bud's heart with your sighs at dawn.[2]
You are lost in your song – because your verse is your tomb:
You did not return to earth because you were not of earth.[3]

PM 330 [373]

[1] *You painted . . . blood:* The tulip is compared to a bride on whose palms the poet-soldier has painted designs, using his own blood for henna.

[2] *And opened . . . dawn:* The poet's songs (called 'sighs' – see below) 'open' the buds' hearts in two senses: (1) they make the buds happy, and (2) they help them become flowers. These songs are born of a feeling heart, as the word 'sighs' suggests, and are sung at dawn – when the poet, possibly alone in the garden, can experience deep feelings and be at his most creative.

[3] *because you were not of earth:* The Persian in the original, *ki tu az zamin na-budi*, simultaneously means 'because you were not made of earth' and 'because you did not belong to earth'.

8

SLAVE CULTURE

As a thinker Iqbal was deeply interested in the phenomenon of the rise and fall of nations. Study and reflection led him to conclude that the responsibility for the decline and disintegration of a nation lay chiefly with that nation itself. This conclusion followed directly from the premise that a nation controls its own destiny. Thus Iqbal had no doubt that Muslims had only themselves to blame for the sorry state in which they found themselves. In his view, one nation is subjugated by another only when it allows this to happen. In other words, every dominant culture has a correlative, which is a slave culture; masters become masters because there are slaves who would accept them as such.

This view, bleak as it seems, is not without an element of hope. If a nation is itself responsible for selling itself into slavery, then it is also capable of liberating itself, because the key to its fate lies with itself. The poems that follow present some of Iqbal's thoughts on the subject of slavery. As will be seen, he approaches the subject from several angles, combining analysis with comment, offering profound insights and, as always, not mincing words.

In 'The Psychology of Slaves' Iqbal says that a slave nation does not necessarily lack genius and creativity, but it is the use it makes of its potentialities that marks it as slave. Servility, in other words, is a state of mind.

'Mastership' makes the point that masters owe their position to slaves who recognise them as masters; and it implies that slaves can choose to throw off the yoke of slavery.

In the satirical poem 'The State of *Barzakh*' Iqbal, using resurrection as a metaphor, says that death puts an end to the life of slaves only, and that living nations triumph over death – and are resurrected. *Barzakh*, literally 'barrier', is the Islamic term for the period between death and resurrection.

'Scorpion Land', in which Iqbal calls slavery the worst conceivable form of torment, is one of the most pungent satires in all his poems.

'Advice to Slaves' (the Urdu title translates literally as 'For Slaves') states Iqbal's view that a nation cannot achieve institutional strength if does not possess a set of firm beliefs.

Iqbal had a clear sense of the importance of his message, but he also felt that the land of his birth – India – was not very hospitable to his message. In 'Gratitude and Complaint' he thanks God for making his voice carry far and beyond India's borders; but the poem also registers a complaint.

THE PSYCHOLOGY OF SLAVES

There are poets, there are scholars, and there are sages –
A nation's days of slavery are not uneventful!
But every one of them – poor creatures![1] – has a single goal,
Though each is unique[2] in the ideas he expounds:
'Better teach the lion to take flight like a deer,
So that the legend of the lion's courage is forgotten!'[3]
They seek to make the slaves feel at ease with their slavery,
Pretending to 'expound and reason things out'.[4]

ZK 652 [602-3]

[1] *poor creatures!* The phrase *Allah ke bande* (literally 'creatures of God') in a context like this one is used pityingly.

[2] *unique:* There may be wordplay involved in the use of the word *yaganah.* Each of these illustrious men is 'unique' in the sense of being unsurpassed in his field, but perhaps also in the sense that he does not agree with anyone else in the exposition of his ideas – being thus 'alone' in holding his particular views – the net result being that these people are at variance with one another, and also a source of dissension and anarchy in society.

[3] *'Better teach . . . forgotten!'* In another short piece, also entitled 'The Psychology of Slaves' (*ZK* 669-70 [620]), Iqbal says:

In the creed of the lions
The chiefs and leaders of the slaves see
Only a philosophy of foxes.

[4] *Pretending to 'expound . . . out':* i.e. they claim to offer fresh and supposedly creative interpretations of the problems faced by their nation, although these interpretations are actually aimed at making slavery palatable to the people. Literally 'Using interpretation of matters as their pretext'.

MASTERSHIP

The present age is really the same old age:
It is either the men of prayer[1] or the politicians who are in charge.
Neither the miracles of those men of prayer
Nor the power of government is the reason for it[2] –
For centuries the people have been used to slavery.
There is no difficulty about being a master
When the people are entrenched deep in slavery.[3]

ZK 655 [605]

[1]*the men of prayer: Ahl-i sajjadah* literally means 'people of the prayer-mat'. In the context of the Indian subcontinent, the word *sajjadah* (prayer-mat) refers to the inherited, and therefore institutionalised, spiritual authority of certain individuals over a large number of followers, usually of a rural background, who owe them unquestioning obedience. The *ahl-i sajjadah* often own large estates, and so enjoy feudal power as well. As a result, they are highly influential not only in local but also in national politics.

[2]*Neither the miracles . . . for it:* i.e. the continued dominance of the men of religion or politicians is due not to any miracles performed by the former or to any governmental authority wielded by the latter, but simply to the fact that the common people themselves have become inured to slavery.

[3]*There is . . . slavery:* In another poem, 'Complaint' (*ZK* 663 [613]), Iqbal says that the people of India are themselves to blame for their servitude. The lines are as follows (the 'crown' in the second line is the British Crown):

What is poor India's fate – who knows? – for up till now
It has been a glittering jewel in some crown!
Its peasant is a corpse that some grave has disgorged –
The corpse's tattered shroud is still inside the ground;
His soul and his body are in pawn:
Alas, neither the residence nor the resident survives!
It is you who became the willing slave of Europe:
My complaint is against you, it is not against Europe!

THE STATE OF *BARZAKH*[1]

THE CORPSE TO ITS GRAVE

What is it, this Resurrection Day?[2]
Of what present is it the future?[3]
O my ancient sleeping-chamber,
What is Resurrection Day?

THE GRAVE

O corpse of a hundred years, don't you know
That every death implies a call for resurrection?[4]

THE CORPSE

A death that implies resurrection –
Such a death does not entrap me!
It is true that I have been dead for a hundred years,
But I am not tired of this dark chamber in the earth.
The soul should once again ride the poor body –
If this is resurrection, then I am not a taker!

A VOICE FROM THE UNSEEN

Death is not for snakes and scorpions,
Or for birds and beasts of prey,
Eternal death is the lot of slave nations alone.[5]
Even Israfil's trumpet[6] cannot bring back to life those
Whose bodies, when they lived, had no souls.
To spring back to life after death – only the free can do that,
Even though all living beings are headed
Into the arms of the grave.

THE GRAVE
(to its corpse)

You vicious creature! In the world you were a slave!
I had failed to understand why my soil was as hot as fire!

Your corpse makes my darkness even darker;
It rips the earth's veil of honour.[7]
Beware, beware a hundred times of a slave's corpse!
O Israfil! O Lord of the universe!
O soul that is chaste and pure!

THE VOICE FROM THE UNSEEN

Resurrection upsets the order of the universe,
But it is this commotion[8] that reveals the secrets of existence.
An earthquake makes mountains fly like clouds,[9]
But it also starts new springs flowing in the valleys.
Total destruction must come before any re-creation –
For in this way the problems of existence are resolved.

THE EARTH

Oh, this eternal death! Oh, this struggle that marks life!
Will this conflict in the world ever end?
Reason cannot free itself from its idols;
The commoners and the elite – all are slaves to Lat and Manat.[10]
How abject Adam – the man with divine attributes[11] – has now become!
That such a world should continue to exist
Is more than heart and eye can bear.
Why does man's night not turn into dawn?

AHU 717-20 [661-4]

[1] *Barzakh:* See note on this poem in the introduction to this chapter.

[2] *Resurrection Day:* The word *qiyamat* (Arabic *qiyamah*) means both 'resurrection' and 'Resurrection Day', and in this poem (and elsewhere) Iqbal plays upon the two meanings.

[3] *Of what present is it the future?* Literally 'Of what today is it the tomorrow?'

[4] *That every . . . resurrection:* i.e. resurrection is the logical corollary of every death, and thus everyone who dies must be resurrected.

[5] *Eternal . . . alone:* Elsewhere Iqbal calls slavery 'a worse kind of death' (*AHU* 738 [677]).

[6] *Israfil's trumpet:* Israfil is the name of the angel who will blow the trumpet on the Last Day, causing all dead beings to come back to life.

[7]*Your corpse . . . honour:* i.e. it disgraces the earth.
[8]*this commotion:* The commotion of the Last Day.
[9]*An earthquake . . . clouds:* A composite image whose elements are drawn from several Qur'anic verses about the Last Day, e.g. 27:88 and 99:1.
[10]*Lat and Manat:* Names of pre-Islamic deities of Arabia. The line means that the whole society has embraced idol-worship.
[11]*Adam – the man of divine attributes:* Adam as God's best creation (Qur'an 17:70) and His deputy (2:30) is supposed to reflect the attributes of his Maker. Cf. also the Sufi advice, *takhallaqu bi-akhlaq Allah* ('Assume the good qualities of God'), and the Biblical concept of the creation of man in God's image.

SCORPION LAND

Slavery kills the heart in the body
It makes the soul a burden to the body,
And brings on the infirmity of age in youth,
Slavery causes the wild lion's teeth to fall out.
It divides one member of society from another
So that everyone clashes with everyone else;
There someone is prostrate, here someone is on his feet,
And its[1] affairs become like an un-led prayer;[2]
Everyone falls out with everyone else,
Everyone with a daily worry of his own.[3]
Slavery makes the man of truth wear a *zunnar*;[4]
It robs his pearl of value,[5]
And his branches bear no leaves even when it is not autumn.
He has nothing in his soul but the fear of death,
He has poor taste – and knowingly drinks poison,
Dead in life, he carries his own corpse on his shoulders.
He has compromised the dignity of life:
Like a donkey he is content with grass and barley.
Consider what he can do, and consider what he cannot do;[6]
Consider how the months and years pass for him.
His days mourn one another,
And move more slowly than the sand in an hour-glass.

A brackish land, all thorns from the poison of scorpions,
Whose ants hunt scorpions and sting dragons,
Whose gale is a fire from hell
And gives a fair wind to the ship of Iblis,
A fire that rolls and meshes into the wind,
One flame intertwined with another,
A fire folded in curling smoke,
With the crash of thunder and the sea's fury,
A fire with battling serpents in its arms,
Serpents with poison-dropping hoods,
A fire whose flame seizes one like a biting dog,
Horrible – its flame alive, its light dead! –
Living a hundred lives in such a dreadful wilderness
Is better than a single moment's slavery!

ZA[7] 460-1 [572-3]

[1]*its:* Society's.

[2]*like an un-led prayer:* Disorganised and without direction. A congregational prayer is led by an *imam* (leader) and is performed by all participants in a harmonious manner. A 'leaderless prayer' (*salat-i bi-imam*) thus signifies disunity.

[3]*Everyone falls out . . . own:* i.e. no two persons share the same concern.

[4]*Slavery . . . zunnar: Zunnar* is the ritual thread worn by Hindu devotees. Iqbal means that slavery turns a monotheist into a worshipper of idols.

[5]*It robs . . . value:* Slavery takes away one's merit, the slave becoming like a shell whose pearl has ceased to have value.

[6]*Consider what . . . do:* The Persian line, *mumkinash bingar muhal-i u nigar*, translates literally as: 'Observe his possibility, observe his impossibility' or 'Observe what he can accomplish, observe what he cannot accomplish' – implying, of course, that such man can accomplish very little, for he possesses no initiative or drive. The words *mumkin* and *muhal* are also philosophical terms, the first meaning 'possible existent', the second 'that which cannot possibly exist', and imply that the slave belongs more in the realm of non-existence than in that of existence.

[7]This passage is taken from *Bandagi-Namah,* an independent work within *Zabur-i 'Ajam.*

ADVICE TO SLAVES

The wisdom of the East and West
Has taught me something that will prove elixir to slaves:
Whether it is religion or philosophy, poverty[1] or kingship –
All take firm beliefs as their base.
The words that a nation speaks are dead and its actions are futile
If its heart is bereft of firm beliefs.

ZK 655-6 [606]

[1] *poverty: Faqr*, a technical term in Iqbal, stands not for poverty in money terms but for a state in which one has risen above all needs and, desiring nothing, has everything. The attendant notions include self-sufficiency and contentment, dignity and pride, and disdain for the paltry 'goods and wares' of the world. As the next line indicates, *faqr* or poverty no less than kingship (and religion no less than philosophy) needs the foundation of a strong faith, since otherwise it will lack authenticity and stability.

9

THE EAGLE

A most significant image in Iqbal's poetry, and probably the best-known, is that of the eagle. 'Live in the world like an eagle, and die like an eagle,' says Iqbal (*JN* 654 [773]). It is therefore important in the study of Iqbal's poetry to understand the eagle motif.

We begin by noting two points. The first is that Iqbal's eagle is a construct. It would be a mistake to analyse his descriptions of the eagle in order to assess their ornithological accuracy. Secondly, we shall often be using the word 'eagle' for the various names Iqbal gives to the bird: *shahin*, *ᶜuqab*, *baz*, *shahbaz*. Metrical constraints often determine what word a poet will use at a particular place, but Iqbal seems deliberately to use these words interchangeably. This kind of usage serves Iqbal's purpose, since it enables him to borrow traits from several members of the same family and produce a unified, composite portrait. These two points can be illustrated with the following examples. At one point (*PM* 343 [391]) Iqbal remarks that such is the fierce pride of the eagle that it disdains to eat dead prey and will only eat prey it has caught live. One might object that this description fits the hawk rather than the eagle, but that would miss the point. He also says (see the poem 'The Eagle' in this chapter) that the eagle is above making nests. This, too, is incorrect, but it makes good sense where it occurs (see n. 9 to the poem).

Iqbal uses the eagle motif in several ways: to offer observations on life and society (freedom transforms a nightingale into an eagle, but slavery turns an eagle into a bat; in the struggle for survival the eagle survives and the partridge dies); to elucidate certain aspects of his own philosophy (only the eagle [intuition] catches live prey [truth], whereas the vulture [reason] has to be content with carrion [falsehood parading as truth]); and, above all, to exhort and motivate his audience to action (Muslims must stop living indolent lives and develop the power to fly like the mountain eagle; Muslim teachers, part of an outdated and decadent educational system, are teaching young eagles how to roll in the dust like chickens). To these ends Iqbal invests his eagle with certain character traits, and so the eagle we are dealing with is the Iqbalian eagle. Iqbal is perhaps the first poet in the Islamic – perhaps in the world – literary tradition – to make an elaborate and consistent use of the eagle to represent character. The very word 'eagle', when mentioned in connection with Iqbal's poetry, conjures up a whole set of distinctive physical, moral and behavioural traits with which Iqbal endows the bird. Among its qualities that he admires and writes about are sharp vision, the ability to soar into the air and rule the skies, swift movement, daring, and love of freedom and action. The cultivation of aquiline traits is thus a prerequisite for success in life.

The first poem in this chapter, 'The *Dervish* of the Kingdom of Birds' (the original title translates as 'The Eagle'), highlights the eagle's 'ascetic' and freedom-loving nature: the eagle shuns the pleasurable but enervating life of the garden, preferring the austere but health-giving environment of the desert. The second poem, 'Beyond the Stars' (the original, a *ghazal*, is untitled) is an exhortation to the eagle to discover new worlds by soaring ever higher. The poem is evidently addressed to an eagle that has lost its nest, and consoling it Iqbal says that there are other realms to explore and conquer. The third poem, 'The Falcon's Advice to its Youngster', is the most complete portrait of the eagle in Iqbal's poetry.

THE *DERVISH* OF THE KINGDOM OF BIRDS

I have turned away from that place on earth[1]
Where sustenance takes the form of grain and water.[2]
The solitude of the wilderness pleases me –
By nature I was always a hermit –
No spring breeze, no one plucking roses, no nightingale,
And no sickness of the songs of love![3]
One must shun the garden-dwellers[4] –
They have such seductive charms![5]
The wind of the desert is what gives
The stroke of the brave youth fighting in battle its effect.[6]
I am not hungry for pigeon or dove –
For renunciation is the mark of an eagle's life.
To swoop, withdraw and swoop again
Is only a pretext to keep up the heat of the blood.
East and West – these belong to the world of the pheasant,[7]
The blue sky – vast, boundless – is mine!
I am the *dervish*[8] of the kingdom of birds –
The eagle does not make nests.[9]

BJ 495 [457]

[1]*place on earth:* The word used in the original is *khakdan*, which ordinarily means 'rubbish dump'. Although it is also used in the simple sense of 'earthly world', as probably intended here, pejorative connotations are not entirely absent.

[2]*Where . . . water:* The word used for 'sustenance' in the original is *rizq*, which in the Qur'an signifies not only ordinary but also spiritual and intellectual food. The eagle criticises the limited definition of *rizq* – in terms of bread and water alone (cf. the well-known New Testament saying, 'Man does not live by bread alone'), and the criticism reflects the Qur'anic view, which Iqbal probably has in mind. In the phrase 'grain and water' (idiomatically 'food and water'; original: *ab-o-danah*), 'grain' is suggestive: grain is used as bait under a trap to catch birds. The eagle is thus expressing disdain for birds that fall for cheap *rizq*.

[3]*No spring . . . love!* The wilderness, fortunately, has none of the distractions of life in a garden. The elements enumerated have double significance. At one level, they are a simple description of three successive events: the spring breeze blows and the garden is filled with flowers; the flower-plucker comes and robs the garden of its beauty; and the nightingale, pining for the rose, sings its plaintive song. At another level, they contain allusions to some of the stock-in-trade of the decadent Urdu poetry of Iqbal's times. The phrase *bimari-i naghmah-i ʿashiqanah* can have three meanings: (1) the sickness characteristic of love songs in Urdu poetry, (2) the sickness which love songs cause in those who listen

to them, and (3) the sickness that leads one to compose such songs. While all three of these meanings may be intended, the last one seems the most relevant.

[4]*the garden-dwellers:* Those who live comfortable lives, as in cities with nice parks and gardens. The line thus alludes to urban life with its amenities, and intends to convey the contrast with the simple, austere life of the wilderness (see next lines), the latter style of living of course being the eagle's preference.

[5]*They have . . . . charms!* The implication is that these charms are artificial.

[6]*The wind . . . effect:* Note the eagle's almost imperceptible transformation into – or rather identification with – the brave youth.

[7]*East . . . pheasant:* Iqbal's eagle transcends the limitations represented by the compass points.

[8]*dervish:* A *dervish* is one who has few needs, is content with what he possesses, and has risen above the temptations of the world; if he is poor, it is because he has chosen to live a life of poverty (see also Chapter 12, section 'Muslims', subsection 'Advice to Muslim Women', quatrain no. 3, n. 1.)

[9]*The eagle . . . nests:* This may be interpreted as meaning that the eagle takes no place as its permanent home.

BEYOND THE STARS

Other worlds exist beyond the stars –
More tests of love are still to come.[1]
This vast space does not lack life –
Hundreds of other caravans are here.
Do not be content with the world of colour and smell,[2]
Other gardens there are, other nests, too.
What is the worry if one nest is lost?
There are other places to sigh and cry for![3]
You are an eagle, flight is your vocation:
You have other skies stretching out before you.
Do not let mere day and night ensnare you,
Other times and places belong to you.
Gone are the days when I was alone in company –
Many here are my confidants now.[4]

BJ 389-90 [353]

[1]*More . . . come:* The connection with the first line is as follows: There are yet other worlds you (eagle) will be required to conquer, and that will put to the test your commitment and devotion – or love, in Iqbal's terminology.

[2]*the world of colour and smell:* The terrestrial world.

[3]*There are . . . cry for!* The words *zaman* ('time') and *makan* ('place') also have Sufi connotations: the time one spends in remembrance of God is sacred time; the stages one rises to in one's quest of spiritual perfection are, likewise, qualitatively superior. Iqbal means that, rather than being content with the temporal-spatial framework of this physical world, one should aspire after higher, spiritual moments and places.

[4]*Gone are . . . now:* A personal postscript which does not seem integrally related to the rest of the poem. It should be remembered, however, that this is a *ghazal*, where individual couplets do not necessarily have to treat the same theme. But there may well be a connection between this and the preceding couplets: the eagle presumably understands Iqbal's message, which gives the poet the assurance that many now share his ideas; there was a time when, even in the midst of people, Iqbal felt himself alone, but that is no longer the case.

THE FALCON'S ADVICE TO ITS YOUNGSTER

You know that in essence all falcons are one –
A mere handful of feathers, but with the heart of a lion.
Conduct yourself well and let your strategy[1] be well considered;
Be daring, maintain your dignity,[2] and hunt big game.[3]
Do not mix with partridges, pheasants, and starlings[4] –
Unless you want them as prey.
What a lowly, fearful lot they are –
They wipe their beaks clean with dust![5]
A falcon that copies the ways of his prey
Becomes prey himself.
Many a predator, descending to earth,
Has perished on associating with grain-eaters.[6]
Guard yourself,[7] and live the life
Of one of good cheer, brave, robust and rugged.
Let the quail have his soft and delicate body;
Grow a vein hard as a deer's horn.
All the joy in the world
Comes from hardship, toil, and fullness of breath.'[8]

What fine advice it was that the eagle gave its son:[9]
A single drop of blood is better than the purest wine![10]
Do not seek out company like the deer or sheep,
But go into seclusion as your ancestors did.[11]
I remember the old falcons' advice:
'Do not make your nest on the branch of a tree.'
We do not make nests in a garden or a field –
We have our own paradise in mountains and deserts.
We regard picking up grain from the ground as an error,
For God has given us the vastness of the skies.
If a bird of noble stock scrapes his feet on the ground,
He becomes more despicable than a house bird.
The kingly falcon uses rocks like a carpet –
Walking on them sharpens his claws.
You are one of the yellow-eyed of the desert,[12]
And, like the *simurgh,*[13] are of noble nature;
You are that noble youth who, on the day of battle,

Plucks out the pupil of the tiger's eye.
You fly with the majesty of angels,
And in your veins is the blood of the *kafuri*[14] falcon.
Under this humpbacked, revolving sky
Eat what you catch, whether it is soft or hard –[15]
Do not take food from the hand of another;
Be good and take advice from the good.[16]

PM 258-60 [272-3]

[1]*strategy:* This translation seeks to combine the two principal (and interrelated) meanings of *tadbir* – counsel or opinion and management or handling of affairs.

[2]*maintain your dignity:* The original contains the word *ghayur*, an adjective meaning one who is high-minded and guards his honour jealously.

[3]*hunt big game:* The original contains the phrase *kalan-gir,* which means one who aims high and is not content with small achievements. Cf. n. 5, below.

[4]*Do not . . . starlings:* Elsewhere Iqbal says that an eagle associating with weaker or smaller birds will lose its eagle's nature while those other birds will not become eagles (*BJ* 443 [408]). Iqbal is far from advocating elitism, something he detested and preached against in both his prose and poetry; he only wishes the eagle to remain true to itself as an eagle.

[5]*They wipe . . . dust!* The above-named birds are content to derive their sustenance from the dusty ground. In other words they have no higher goals in life. Cf. n. 3, above.

[6]*grain-eaters:* Ordinary birds, like those mentioned earlier in the text.

[7]*Guard yourself:* The Persian phrase *nigah dar khud ra* has a moral ring to it. The meaning is: monitor yourself, guard your virtue and avoid evil.

[8]*fullness of breath:* This is the literal translation of the Persian word used, *pur-dami,* and it connotes indefatigableness.

[9]*What fine . . . son:* This line is an interjection by the poet.

[10]*A single . . . wine!* The blood of a bird will keep you fit and strong, whereas wine will make you effete. Note that the word here translated as wine (more precisely, it is red wine) is *la'l* in the original, which can also mean 'gem, ruby', but since it is qualified by *nab* (pure), it is better rendered as wine. Furthermore, the eagle's statement is better understood as contrasting one kind of drink (blood) with another (wine). It goes without saying that wine is here a metaphor for an easy, carefree life, and that Iqbal is not suggesting that eagles drink wine.

[11]*Do not . . . ancestors did:* Do not cultivate the herd instinct, but learn to withdraw into your own self, as your ancestors did, so that you can bring out your potential.

[12]*the yellow-eyed of the desert:* Desert hawks.

[13]*simurgh:* A legendary bird. In the long Sufi allegorical poem *Mantiq at-Tayr* by Farid ad-Din ʿAttar (d. 1220), a group of birds, wishing to have a king of

their own like all other species, set out in search of the *simurgh*, their would-be king. The name thus comes to have connotations of royalty and majesty.

[14]*kafuri:* Iqbal explains the word in a note: 'A white hunting bird of the type of falcon found in the mountains and deserts of Turkestan.'

[15]*whether it is soft or hard:* Whether it is palatable and delicious or not.

[16]Another poem, entitled 'Advice' (again by an eagle to its young offspring), occurs in *Bal-i Jibril*, 448 [412]. It is short enough to be quoted here in full:

> The old eagle said to its youngster:
> 'May the heights of the lofty sky be easy on your wings!
> Youth means burning in one's own blood:
> It is hard work that turns life's bitter into sweet.
> My son, perhaps the delight of swooping down on the pigeon
> Is not to be found in the pigeon's own blood.'

10

FABLES AND AETIOLOGIES

In several of Iqbal's poems animal characters hold brief dialogues. Typically one animal makes a remark – in the form of an assertion, a question, or some information – to which the other animal responds with either a positive or a negative comment, an explanation or a correction. While such poems in themselves are not difficult to understand, a little reflection on their content shows that Iqbal uses them to illustrate deeper ideas. Each poem takes up a theme that is essentially moral, and deals with it in such a way that we can clearly see Iqbal's position. These 'fable poems' (the first five in this chapter) summarise aspects of his philosophy of life which he treats in detail elsewhere.

A central idea in Iqbal's philosophy is *khudi*. Literally 'selfhood', *khudi* may be described – at the risk of over-using the word 'self' – as self-affirmation, self-reliance, self-expression, self-discipline and self-fulfilment. The first five poems can all be seen as addressing aspects of *khudi*. In 'The Lion and the Mule' (which, as Iqbal mentions, is adapted from a German original), the mule is suffering from an identity crisis. Asked by the lion to identify himself by naming his parents, the mule is unable, or rather too ashamed, to do so in plain words but alludes instead to the horse, his maternal uncle, as possessing great virtue. The poem illustrates the Persian saying, *Pidaram sultan bud* (My father was a king!), which criticises the mentality of those who, unable to point to any achievement of their own, take false pride in being the offspring of one better known.

The same point is made in a slightly different way by 'The Moth and the Firefly'. The moth criticises the firefly because its glow is flameless. But the moth itself, as the firefly duly reminds it, is dependent on an external source for light: it circles the lamp like a beggar, seeking 'alien' fire, something which the firefly's strong sense of *khudi* would not permit it to do.

According to Iqbal, human beings submit to God, but nature submits to human beings – an Islamic concept expressed by the

Qur'anic term *taskhir.* This signifies, on the one hand, God's harnessing of nature in the service of human beings, and, on the other, the conquest of nature by human beings for their own use and benefit. In other words, human beings are expected to become masters of the universe, and this is the lesson of the next poem, 'The Young Fish and the Eaglet'. The young fish, enveloped as it is by sea water, is overawed by the compelling power of its environment. The eaglet, however, not only refuses to be circumscribed by its environment, but insists on asserting its dominance over it. Unlike the young fish which has allowed its *khudi* to be submerged – both literally and figuratively – in the sea, the eaglet has guarded its *khudi* and is thus able to rise – again both literally and figuratively – above all limitations.

Iqbal's study of world politics had convinced him that power could be countered only with power, and that the appeal to morality or good sense, which is typically made by the weak, goes unheeded by the strong. Iqbal takes up this subject in many poems, approaching it from different angles. In 'The Duck and the Crocodile' (the original title translates as 'Freedom of the Seas') the problem is briefly stated. The duck requests the crocodile, for which it is no match, to allow it freedom of the waters. The crocodile gives a qualified consent: the duck may go wherever it likes, but should not forget that it is always within the crocodile's reach. In other words, the freedom enjoyed by the duck is illusory. While Iqbal is certainly not on the side of the crocodile, he does not consider the duck entirely blameless either, and probably has little sympathy for it. In several other poems Iqbal remarks that weakness is a sin whose 'wages' is death (e.g., *BJ* 487 [449]), and that the most fatal weakness is weakness of *khudi*. 'The Duck and the Crocodile' aptly illustrates this lesson.

There is a certain category of fables that purports to explain, for example, how the elephant came to have a trunk or the centipede so many legs. These may be called 'aetiological' fables, and in a sense 'The Ant and the Eagle' is one of them. Iqbal seems to suggest that an ant is an ant because it is content to remain in a lowly condition – it has allowed its *khudi* to rot and rust – whereas the eagle is the king of birds because it has preserved its *khudi* and thus possesses irrepressible inner drive and energy. Again, it is the presence or absence of *khudi* that sets the eagle apart from the fish.

'The Ant and the Eagle' brings us to aetiology proper. The last two poems in this chapter are expressly aetiological, and give evidence of both Iqbal's imaginative power and his artistic skill.

In 'The Perfume of the Flower' Iqbal explains how the perfume of the flower (or the rose [*gul*]) came to be so called. The poem begins with a houri of paradise desiring to know the truth about the world of day and night, and of birth and death – in other words, the terrestrial world ruled by the laws of change. She wafts her way into the world as perfume, takes up residence in the stem of a flower, becomes first a bud and then a flower, and finally (since she has entered the world of time and thus become subject to the law of death) dies, her petals dropping to the ground and withering away. But before dying she utters a sigh, and this sigh, her memorial, receives the name of perfume.

The 'disquiet' of the houri mentioned in the poem's opening line represents Iqbal's own dissatisfaction with the notion of static perfection. If paradise is only to be understood as a perfect abode in the sense that it lacks movement and growth, it would, in Iqbal's view, be a place unworthy of habitation, and in several other places (e.g. 'The Houri and the Poet', Chapter 6) he says that an eternal and changeless paradise would kill the 'hearts of lovers' – i.e. those in love with an unattainably high and noble ideal. Endless progress, limitless improvement – that is what Iqbal desires, and the houri understandably becomes impatient with paradisal existence. The terrestrial world, despite its imperfections, is interesting and charming enough, and Iqbal seems to be suggesting that the houri's decision to descend to earth was not wrong. To be sure, she pays a heavy price for it; one is tempted to compare her to Faust because it is her love of discovery, her hunger to understand the truth of the alteration of day and night and the phenomena of birth and death, and her willingness to indulge her fancy at any cost, that causes her to quit paradise and enter this world. For the discoveries she makes and the understanding she acquires she pays with her life. This is exactly what befalls Faust (cf. Chapter 6, 'The Houri and the Poet', n. 38).

The houri breathes a sigh as she leaves this world – when, as Iqbal puts it (see n. 5), her feet are 'unshackled'. What does the sigh signify? The poem does not provide a clear answer, and the ambiguity may be deliberate. Did the houri sigh because she would soon cease to exist altogether, and felt that she had paid too big a price to satisfy her curiosity? Or was it the case that she liked this imperfect and transient world regardless of the consequences she had to suffer for choosing to live in it, and was filled with regret on departing from it?

In 'Love' Iqbal suggests that love is like the soul to the body of the universe: the world, at the time of its creation, was like a frozen picture that became animated only when it was infused with love. Not only did love transform a static world into a dynamic one, but it also gave meaning and purpose to existence itself. It is noteworthy that Iqbal associates love with God: the secret recipe of love which the heavenly alchemist wished to acquire was inscribed on one of the uprights of the divine Throne and closely guarded by the angels. God did not, however, intervene when the alchemist approached the Throne under the pretext of glorifying Him, thus 'tricking' the angelic guard. This can only mean that God wanted the secret discovered. Moreover, it was God Himself who gave the name Love to the compound prepared by the alchemist.

Two questions arise about the poem. First, who is the heavenly alchemist? In one way he resembles Prometheus, who stole fire and gave it as a gift to humanity. But he cannot be identified completely with Prometheus, who was punished by Zeus, whereas the alchemist's action has divine approval. In another sense the alchemist is like Khizr, the name traditionally given to the person who guided the prophet Moses on a certain journey as described in the 18th *surah* of the Qur'an. Note especially that Iqbal calls the alchemist 'a confidant of the Court of God', which invites comparison with the Qur'anic description of the guide of Moses as 'one of Our servant-worshippers' and as one whom God had blessed with special insight (18:65). Furthermore, the alchemist dissolves the ingredients of the recipe 'in the water of the fountain of life', and the Islamic literary tradition represents Khizr as having discovered and drunk from the fountain of life. In yet another sense it might be argued that, alchemy – or chemistry – being one of the distinctive Muslim contributions to science, the alchemist is a typical representative of Islamic civilisation. But while Iqbal's alchemist has traits or qualities of Prometheus, Khizr and a scientist, he cannot be identified fully and exclusively with any one of them and must be regarded as a composite figure created by Iqbal.

The second question is: what is meant in this poem by love? This may be answered in two ways. Love is constituted of ingredients listed in detail in the poem. What is notable is that these ingredients are strongly reminiscent of the descriptions of the lover and the beloved in Persian-Urdu poetry. In this literary tradition the beloved is often described as having a bright, star-like face and long pitch-black hair, and possessing the modesty of a houri and Jesus-like power to revive the pining and near-dead lover with an affectionate look and a kind word, but showing godlike indifference to him. The lover, on the other hand, is described as humble and self-sacrificing, for ever hoping to win the favour of his beloved. Iqbal thus employs the native literary tradition in the service of a philosophical idea whose import, as we shall see, is universal.

As for its function, love, as we learn in the concluding lines of the poem, is the principle of movement in the universe – the bond that unites the atoms of the universe, sets the heavenly bodies in motion, and makes the flowers bloom. This does not seem to help much, but then it is not meant to be a scientific answer to a scientific question. Iqbal, it seems, is trying to present a philosophical idea in poetic language. The universe is a unity: the heavenly bodies on the one hand and the flowers in earthly gardens on the other are parts of the same system and are ruled by what are essentially the same laws. All phenomena are thus interlinked, together making up a system remarkable for its harmony. Harmony, then, is the underlying principle of the universe – and another word for this harmony is love. Just as scientists are trying to discover an ultimate principle that would bring out the unity of the physical universe, so the philosopher searches for a principle that would reveal the spiritual basis of that unity. This, one might say, is the 'stone' the philosopher is in search of.

We are told that while the recipe of love was in the heavens, the ingredients of the recipe were to be found on earth. This is significant because it implies on the one hand that love is 'earthly' in character and on the other that earthly love is sanctioned by heaven. And that is not all. Once the alchemist succeeds in preparing the compound called love – a name given by God Himself – the whole universe becomes ready to function. Love, in other words, knits the heavens and the earth into a unity; it is to the universe what the soul is to the body.

THE LION AND THE MULE

THE LION

You are so different and unlike
All the other dwellers of the wild and the desert!
Who are your parents and ancestors?
And what is your tribe?

THE MULE

Perhaps your highness does not know
My uncle – my mother's brother:
He gallops like the wind, and is
The pride of the royal stable![1]

BJ 498-9 [460-1]

[1] *Perhaps your . . . royal stable!* The mule shows surprise at the lion's ignorance: if the lion had known the horse at all, he would have easily noticed the resemblance between the two relatives. The mule's surprise is of course faked, and meant to hide his sense of shame.

THE MOTH AND THE FIREFLY

THE MOTH

The firefly is so far removed
From the status of the moth!
Why is it so proud
Of a fire that cannot burn?

THE FIREFLY

God be thanked a hundred times,
That I am not a moth –
That I am no beggar
Of alien fire![1,2]

BJ 442 [407]

[1] *That I am no . . . fire!* Or: 'That I don't beg fire of others'.
[2] *God be thanked . . . fire!* In another short poem entitled 'The Firefly' (*PM* 272 [287]) the same thought is expressed:

I heard a firefly saying:
'I am not an ant whose sting
Would make anyone cry.
It is possible to burn
Without being in debt to others;
Do not think that my creed is that of a moth.
Even if the night is darker than the deer's eye,
I light myself up –
I myself am the lamp of my path.'

THE YOUNG FISH AND THE EAGLET

A sprightly young fish said to an eaglet:
'This succession of waves that you see
Is a single sea, and it contains
Crocodiles that bellow more loudly than thunder clouds;
Its chest is a storehouse
Of hazards and dangers known and unknown.
Its huge flood travels swiftly and covers the land;
It has sparkling diamonds and lustrous pearls.[1]
One cannot escape its all-enveloping flood:
Above our heads, under our feet – it is everywhere!
Young and for ever coursing along!
Revolutions of time have not added to it
Or diminished it.'[2]
The young fish spoke with passion and zest,
Its face beamed as it spoke.[3]
The eaglet laughed. From the shore it rose
Into the air, saying out loud:
'I am an eagle, what have I to do with earth?
Sea or desert – everything is under our wings!'
Leave the water,
Befriend the vastness of space![4]
Only an observant eye
Will see the point of it.[5]

PM 271 [286-7]

[1]*Its huge . . . pearls:* The sea has great destructive force, but it also yields precious pearls. The young fish is trying to impress the eaglet with the wonders of the sea.

[2]*Revolutions . . . diminished it:* Time has not changed the mighty sea in any way.

[3]*The young . . . beamed:* The young fish's pride in identifying itself with the sea is only too obvious.

[4]*Leave the water . . . space!* In this poem freedom is associated with space, and limitation with the earth and sea. Quite appropriately, then, the fish represents water and the eaglet space.

[5]*Only an observant . . . it:* i.e. the point of the advice 'Leave . . . space'. There is possible wordplay in the use of the expression *didah-i bina* ('the seeing eye'; the actual phrase used is: . . . *an didah ki bina'st*) which here means both

'sight' and 'insight': only one possessed of deep insight can 'see' the truth of Iqbal's statement about the water and air—just as its keen sight enables the eagle to 'see' the difference between the sea and the skies. Iqbal, in other words, wishes those whom he addresses to develop the vision of an eagle.

THE DUCK AND THE CROCODILE

A duck said, 'The lanes of the sea are now free! –
The edict from the court of Khizr says so!'[1]
A crocodile said, 'Go anywhere you like,
But never forget to watch out for us!'

PM 338 [387]

[1]*Khizr:* Khizr – in the original Khizar (Arabic Khidr) – is a legendary figure venerated in folk literature as the 'patron saint' of the waters and in Sufi literature as one possessed of special knowledge and powers. He is sometimes identified with the man who, according to Qur'an 18:65 ff., was appointed by God to instruct Moses in certain aspects of the divine administration of the universe. See also Chapter 3, 'Gabriel and Iblis', n. 13.

THE ANT AND THE EAGLE

THE ANT

I am so miserable and forlorn –
Why is your station loftier than the skies?

THE EAGLE

You forage about in dusty paths;
The nine heavens are as nothing to me!

BJ 499 [461]

THE PERFUME OF THE FLOWER

In a bower of heaven's garden,
A houri became anxious and said:
'No one ever told us about the region
On that side of the heavens.[1]
I do not understand
About day and night, morning and evening,
And I am at my wits' end
When they talk about birth and death.'[2]
She became a waft of perfume
And emerged from a flower-branch;
Thus she set foot
In the world of yesterday and tomorrow.[3]
She opened her eyes,
Became a bud, and for a time smiled;
She turned into a flower,
Which soon withered and crumbled to the ground.
The memory of that lovely maiden –
Her feet unshackled[4] –
Is kept alive
By that sigh of hers which is called perfume.

PM 247-8 [259]

[1]*the region . . . heavens:* The terrestrial world.
[2]*I do not understand . . . death:* All these things are foreign to the houri's experience.
[3]*the world of yesterday and tomorrow:* The world of historical time.
[4]*Her feet unshackled:* This is a simple metaphor for death, and does not necessarily connote release from a life which is regarded as imprisonment.

LOVE

The tresses of the bride of night were still uncurled;[1]
The stars of the sky knew nothing of the joy of travel;
The moon in its new apparel looked strange,
And was still ignorant of the iron law that makes it revolve;[2]
It was not long since the world had emerged
From the dark chamber of possibilities;[3]
The vast universe had no appreciation of life.[4]
One could say that the order of existence
Was in the first stages of perfection:
The eye of the ring had an evident desire for a stone.[5]
It is said that high up in the world[6]
There was an alchemist,
And the dust under his feet as he walked
Was purer than the cup of Jamshed.[7]
On one of the uprights of the Throne was inscribed
The recipe of an elixir[8] which the angels kept hidden
From the eye of Adam's soul.[9]
But the alchemist was always on the lookout;
That recipe was worth more to him
Than the Most High Name.[10]
He moved towards the Throne,
On the pretext of glorifying God,
And finally, through resolute effort,
He obtained his heart's desire.
The search for ingredients
Made him roam the field of possibilities[11] –
How could anything stay hidden
From a confidant of the Court of God![12]
From the star he borrowed some glitter,
From the moon the scar in its heart;[13]
From the night's ruffled tresses
He pulled out some black hairs;
From the lightning he took its flash,
Chastity from the houri,
And warmth from the breath

Of Jesus the son of Mary.[14]
Then from God he took
A pinch of sublime unconcern;[15]
He took humility from the angels,
And self-abasement from the dew.
All these ingredients he dissolved
In the water of the fountain of life.
From the Grand Throne
The compound received the name Love.
The alchemist sprinkled this water
On the new and fresh order of existence.
It was as if his skill was untying the knot
Of the world's affairs.[16]
Movement appeared:
The atoms gave up the joys of slumber,
And got up and began to embrace each other;
The suns and the stars received their proud gait;
The buds learnt how to bloom,
And the tulip-beds acquired their scars.

BD 137–8 [111–2]

[1]*The tresses . . . uncurled:* The night is portrayed here as a bride who did not yet know how to curl her hair. In other words, it had not yet acquired the charm peculiar to it.

[2]*And was still . . . revolve:* The moon was unaware that its lot was to be constant orbiting.

[3]*It was not . . . possibilities:* The world, in Muslim theological and philosophical terminology, is possible and contingent, whereas God is the only necessary and absolute being.

[4]*The vast . . . life:* This was so because true appreciation of life would only come after love had informed the universe.

[5]*The eye . . . stone:* The eye of a ring is the rim of metal in which a stone is set. That the eye of the ring was in need of a stone means that the world was still imperfect and yearned for perfection. But the stone that would make the ring complete had yet to be supplied.

[6]*high up in the world:* In the heavenly realm (*ᶜalam-i bala*).

[7]*And the dust . . . Jamshed:* Jamshed, a king of ancient Persia, is said to possess a crystal bowl in which he could see all that was happenings in the world; but for him to be able to do so the cup had to be shiny and clear. The dust of the ground on which the alchemist walked was, however, brighter or clearer (the word *safa* denotes purity, which in turn suggests clarity,

transparency, brightness in this context) than Jamshed's cup. Incidentally, this line may contain an allusion to Qur'an 20:96. When Moses returned from Mount Sinai and learnt that his people had taken to worshipping a calf, he interrogated the Samaritan who had made it. The Samaritan tried to excuse himself by saying that he had seen Gabriel pass by and, taking a handful of dust from the angel's path, cast it into the calf's body, and this made the calf speak. Iqbal, of course, does not mean to compare the Samaritan of *Surah* 20 to the alchemist of his poem – the Samaritan is evil whereas the alchemist is a hero – but on a purely linguistic level the Qur'anic phrase *fa-qabadtu qabdatan min athari r-rasuli* of 20:96 may have suggested 'the dust under his feet' of Iqbal's poem.

[8]*elixir:* Elixir of love (see below).

[9]*the eye of Adam's soul:* The phrase implies that Adam had not yet assumed bodily form.

[10]*the Most High Name:* One of the names of God, although it is not certain which one; on being uttered, it is supposed to produce miraculous effects.

[11]*the field of possibilities:* The terrestrial world, which is marked by contingency or possibility.

[12]*a confidant of the Court of God!* A possible comparison with Khizr (see introduction to this chapter).

[13]*from the moon . . . heart:* It is implied that the moon received its scar from the fire of love which burned in its heart. The scar represents the mark of love in a lover's heart, and so has positive rather than pejorative connotations.

[14]*And warmth . . . Mary:* Jesus had the special gift of reviving the dead. Love is thus a positive, life-giving force, the animating principle of the universe.

[15]*sublime unconcern:* See the introduction to this chapter.

[16]*his skill . . . affairs:* 'To untie the knot' of something is to remove what prevents it from moving or progressing. The world, although it had come into existence, had yet to become 'operational'. Once informed by love, it was stimulated into action and became vibrant with life.

11
MISCELLANEA

Of the five poems in this chapter the first two are about Islam's past glory. The Mediterranean island of Sicily was under Muslim rule from the ninth to the eleventh century. Iqbal was able to see the island from a distance while sailing through the Mediterranean (hence the line in the first poem: 'There is the tomb of Arabian civilisation!'), and the sight made him deeply nostalgic. Recalling that other poets have written songs of mourning about other cities (a few are mentioned in the poem), Iqbal takes it upon himself to write one about Sicily. He identifies himself completely with Muslim Sicily, and wishes it well – in terms reminiscent of ancient Arabic poetry, where the poet-lover greets the ruins which were once the dwelling-place of his beloved. But his pain and sorrow are unmitigated, and in the end he remains uncomforted.

Thoughts of Andalusia – the heart of Muslim Spain – also filled Iqbal with nostalgia and led him to compose some beautiful poems (including the long 'Cordoba Mosque' in *Bal-i Jibril*, generally considered his masterpiece). The second poem in this chapter is about Muᶜtamid, about whom Iqbal writes this introductory note: 'Muᶜtamid was the king of Seville and a poet of Arabic. A Spanish ruler [the Almoravid Yusuf b. Tashufin] had defeated and imprisoned him. His poems, in English translation, have been published in the "Wisdom of the East" series'. The short poem, like the first one, is full of pathos, but here the pathos is controlled. The most poignant moment is when Muᶜtamid, analysing his own situation, remarks that his sword and his chains may have been made of the same metal. The remark also illustrates a favourite theme of Iqbal's – namely that liberty and honour can only be preserved through constant vigilance, that to rest on one's laurels is to invite disaster, since the very sword that can make one master of the world will, if given up, turn into one's chains.

'Fatimah bint ᶜAbdullah' (*bint* means 'daughter [of]'), written in 1912, commemorates an event during the battle of Tripoli

(Libya). Fatimah, as the Urdu subtitle of the poem explains, was a young Arab girl who was martyred while offering water to Muslim soldiers defending their country against the Italian invasion. The notable thing is that Iqbal turns a song of mourning into one of celebration. Fatimah died, but she set a heroic example. Iqbal finds comfort in the thought that even today the Muslim community can give birth to models of courage like Fatimah. Such a community has no cause to despair; it has every reason to live in hope.

The last two poems represent two contrasting moods of the poet-thinker. 'The Pen of Fate' is bleak and pessimistic: the world seems to have exhausted its possibilities, and no signs of creativity can be seen anywhere – it is as if the Pen of Fate itself is too weary to write any further. The 'Vision of a New World' on the other hand strikes an optimistic, perhaps idealistic, note – the piece is prefatory to a long disquisition, in *Javid Namah*, by the modern Muslim reformer Jamal ad-Din al-Afghani (1839-97). The vision, which is as much Iqbal's as it is Afghani's, is at one and the same time intellectual, ethical, religious and humanistic. It is intellectual in that it seeks to achieve a viable balance between the principles of constancy and change; it rests on an enduring substratum that, on the one hand, guarantees continuity in society and, on the other, supports an institutional framework which is responsive to society's changing needs. It is ethical in that it is marked by egalitarianism; it does not divide humankind into oppressors and victims, but erases all artificial barriers that exist among the members of the human race. It is religious in that it finds its historical sanction in a religion – Islam. According to Iqbal, the rule of the second caliph of Islam, ʿUmar, represents an objectification of the ideal outlined here. Finally, the vision is humanistic in that the most important material needed for the building of the ideal world is human material: it is human will and aspirations that will bring such a world into existence. The ideal world thus exists within us, and only has to be brought out and given tangible form.

SICILY

Cry your heart out, eyes of mine,
That are weeping tears of blood!
There is the tomb of Arabian civilisation!
Once this place was full of commotion
Because of those desert-dwellers[1]
Whose ships sported the ocean as if it were a playground,
Who made the courts of kings quake,
And in whose swords dwelt lightning;
They were harbingers of a new world –
Their restless sword devoured the Old Era.[2]
They revived the dead world with the call of 'Rise!'[3] –
Releasing man from the fetters of superstition.
Their resounding call – 'God is the Greatest!'[4] –
Is still music to the ears – is that call now stilled for ever?
Sicily! You are the pride and honour of the seas.
You are like a guide in this desert of water.
May your beauty spot for ever adorn the ocean's cheek,
And may your lights reassure the mariner.
May your scenes for ever be pleasing to the traveller's eye,
And the waves for ever dance on the rocks round your shore.
You once nurtured the civilisation of that nation
Whose world-inflaming beauty dazzled the beholders' eyes.[5]

The nightingale of Shiraz lamented over Baghdad;[6]
Dagh wept tears of blood over Jahanabad;[7]
And, when the heavens destroyed the state of Granada,
The grieving heart of Ibn-i Badrun cried out in pain.[8]
A sorrowful Iqbal must carry out the duty of mourning you –
Fate chose a heart that was your intimate.
Whose is the story that your remains conceal?
The silence of your shores is as eloquent as speech.
Speak to me of your sorrow – I too am sorrowful.
I am the dust of the caravan that came to you as its destination.[9]
Add colour to that old picture and show it to me;
Tell the story of old times and fire me with longing.

I will carry your gift all the way to India:
Here I myself weep – there I will make others do so.

BD 159 [133-4]

[1]*desert-dwellers:* Arabs, or rather Arab Muslims.

[2]*the Old Era:* The era of oppressive political rule and unjust social and economic order.

[3]*They revived . . . 'Rise!'* They possessed power akin to that of Jesus to bring a dead world back to life.

[4]*'God is the Greatest!'* The Arabic phrase *Allahu Akbar* is an Islamic formulaic utterance used in the call to prayer, and in the prayer itself. The actual word used in the text is *takbir*, which means 'to say *Allahu Akbar*'.

[5]*Whose world-inflaming . . . eyes:* An allusion to the divine epiphany on Mount Sinai, mentioned in Qur'an 7:143, according to which God, responding to the request of Moses, manifested Himself on the mountain, crushing it to pieces, with Moses falling unconscious. In other words, the 'beauty' of the Arab nation partook of Divine Beauty.

[6]*The nightingale . . . Baghdad:* Muslihuddin Sa[c]di of Shiraz (*c.* 1210-92) was one of Persia's greatest poets. In his verse he mourned the destruction of Baghdad (1258) at the hands of the Mongols.

[7]*Dagh . . . Jahanabad:* Jahanabad (or Shahjahanabad), the so-called seventh city of Delhi, was named after Shah Jahan, the Mughal emperor who founded it. Delhi, the seat of the Mughal Empire, was occupied by the British in 1857, the year in which a revolt (called a 'mutiny' by them and a 'war of independence' by the Indian Muslims) against the British led to large-scale destruction of life and property. Nawwab Mirza Khan, known by his pen-name Dagh (1831-1905), wrote a threnody commemorating the events of 1857.

[8]*And, when . . . pain:* The threnody on Granada, which fell in 1492, was actually written by Ibn-i [c]Abdun (in Arabic, Ibn [c]Abdun). Ibn-i Badrun (in Arabic, Ibn Badrun) was the commentator on the work.

[9]*I am . . . destination:* Iqbal calls himself a member (but one left far behind, like the dust) of the caravan of Islamic civilisation.

MU^cTAMID'S LAMENT IN PRISON

In my breast,
A wail of grief,
Without any spark or flash,
Alone survives,
Passionless, ineffectual.
A free man is in prison today,
Without a spear or a sword;
Regret overwhelms me
And also my strategy.[1]
My heart
Is drawn by instinct to chains.
Perhaps my sword was of the same steel.
Once I had a two-edged sword –
It turned into the chains that shackle me now.
How whimsical and indifferent
Is the Author of fates.

BJ 428-9 [393-4]

[1] *And also my strategy: Tadbir,* the word used in the original for 'strategy', has several meanings: counsel, policy, management of affairs, strategy. Mu^ctamid says that his strategy failed, that he did not succeed in averting his fate by anything he did or planned.

FATIMAH BINT ᶜABDULLAH

Fatimah, you are the pride
Of the Community – God bless it!
Your dust is holy,[1] every particle of it.
You, houri of the desert,
Were fated to win such merit!
To give the soldiers of Islam water to drink
Was to be your good fortune.
A *jihad* [2] in the way of God,
Waged without sword or shield!
What courage the love of martyrdom gives!
O that in our autumn-stricken garden
There were flower-buds like this!
O that a spark like this, dear Lord,
Could be found in our ashes!
In our desert many deer still hide!
And in the spent clouds
Many flashes of lightning still lie dormant!

Fatimah, though our grieving eyes
Weep tears like dew over you,
Our dirge is also a celebration song.
How thrilling is the dance of your dust,
Every atom of which is charged with life.
There is stirring in your quiet grave:
Within it a new nation is being reared.
Though I know nothing of the range of its[3] ambition,
I see them spring to life from this tomb.
New stars are appearing in the sky above,
Stars whose rolling waves of light
Have not been seen[4] by the eyes of man;
Stars just risen out of the dark dungeon of time,
Stars whose light is not hostage to day and night; [5]
Stars whose radiance is both old and new,
And partakes of the splendour
Of the star of your destiny too.

BD 243-4 [214-5]

[1]*holy:* The word *ma'sum* in the original has the twin senses of 'guiltless' and 'guileless'. It may be translated as 'pure', but perhaps 'holy' is more appropriate.
[2]*jihad:* War in the way of God.
[3]*its:* The (new) nation's.
[4]*Have not been seen: Na-mahram,* the word used in the original, connotes chastity: the waves of light are pure like women who have been shielded from men's looks.
[5]*Stars whose . . . night:* They are not like stars that shine in the night only and vanish at daybreak. In other words, they will shine for ever.

PRAYER

Lord, fill the Muslim's heart
With a desire so fervent[1]
That it will set his heart aflame
And stir his soul.
Light up again every speck of dust
In the Valley of Faran.[2]
Make us long again for beautiful sights,
And create in us the urge to make demands.[3]
Give piercing vision
To those deprived of sight,
And show to others what I have seen.[4]
Lead the stray gazelle back to the Sanctuary.[5]
It has grown used to the city –
Give it back the vastness of the desert.[6]
Stir up again the ruins of the heart
With a commotion like Judgment Day.[7]
Let this empty litter[8] once again seat
A sweetheart – a Layla![9]
In the darkness of this age give
To every troubled heart
Scars of love that would shame the moon.[10]
Let the goals be as high as the Pleiades.
Give us the calm and poise of the shore,
But the freedom of the sea.[11]
Let love be selfless
And truth fearless;
Let our breasts be flooded with light –
Make our hearts clear as crystal.[12]
Enable us to foresee the calamity that is coming;[13]
In the midst of today's upheaval
Give us a vision of tomorrow.[14]
I am a nightingale making my lament,
I am from a garden which has been ravaged.[15]
I wish that my prayer would have effect –
Give to a beggar, bounteous Lord!

BD 241-2 [212-3]

[1]*Lord . . . fervent:* As in many other poems, Iqbal here prays that Muslims may be fired with ambition so that they will shake off their lethargy and be moved to action. That way they will regain their lost glory. *Zindah tamanna* ('fervent desire') is, literally, 'living desire'.

[2]*the Valley of Faran:* Mecca, or Arabia. Mecca lies in a valley between mountains which make up the Faran range.

[3]*Make us . . . demands:* The allusion is to the request by Moses, made with some insistence (hence 'the urge to make demands'), to see God with his own eyes (Qur'an 7:143). This demand was a bold one. Iqbal wants Muslims to cultivate the Mosaic quality of setting high goals and persevering to achieve them.

[4]*And show . . . seen:* Give to others the insights I possess.

[5]*Lead . . . Sanctuary:* The gazelle is the Muslim, the Sanctuary is the Kaᶜbah. To say that the gazelle is lost means that Muslims have forgotten their true vocation; and to say that the gazelle should be taken back to the Sanctuary means that Muslims should be reoriented towards pristine Islam.

[6]*It has grown . . . desert:* Iqbal uses 'city' as a metaphor for a comfortable but passive existence, and 'desert' as a metaphor for one that is simple but dynamic. City life represents the encroachment of the material on the spiritual, and the artificial on the natural; it dulls the senses, impoverishes the instincts, and strait-jackets what ought to be free and uncircumscribed. The Muslim – the gazelle of the verse – has become used to a life of ease and comfort, and so needs to be taken back to an environment that will revive his spirit and develop his latent capacities. In other words, Muslims must give up their indolent ways, rededicate themselves to the cause of Islam, and, by drawing on their authentic religious and spiritual heritage, rediscover themselves.

[7]*With a . . . Day:* i.e. by bringing about a thoroughgoing change.

[8]*litter: Mahmil* is a couch, usually canopied, on the back of an animal, used for riding.

[9]*A sweetheart – a Layla!* Layla, the famous beloved of Majnun in the Arabic folk and literary tradition, travelled in a camel-borne *mahmil.* Iqbal compares the Muslim's heart, which is without ambition, to an empty litter, and prays that it may be filled with an ardent desire to pursue high ideals.

[10]*give . . . the moon:* 'Love' stands for devotion to a noble cause, sufficiently deep to make a permanent imprint (what Iqbal calls 'scars') on minds and hearts. Poets often mention the moon in contexts of love. The shadows in the moon set Iqbal thinking of the scars in the heart of a pining lover, and he prays that love may leave on the hearts and minds of Muslims a deeper imprint than the one it has left on the moon.

[11]*Give us . . . sea:* The shore stays in its place – it 'holds its ground' – and can thus be thought of as self-possessed. But it lacks the freedom of movement enjoyed by the waves of the sea. Iqbal wants Muslims to have both serene dignity and complete freedom.

[12]*Make . . . crystal:* Literally 'Give hearts that are like a decanter'. A decanter is made of glass, and the glass is supposed to be clear and transparent so that

the colour of the wine in the decanter can be seen. In praying thus, Iqbal asks that hearts should be true and sincere.

[13]*Enable us . . . coming:* Give us foresight, so that we can anticipate our problems and take precautions against disaster.

[14]*In the midst . . . tomorrow:* Do not let our present problems overwhelm us, but give us the ability to think ahead and plan for a better future.

[15]*I am from . . . ravaged:* Iqbal calls himself a sorrow-stricken representative of the once glorious Islamic civilisation.

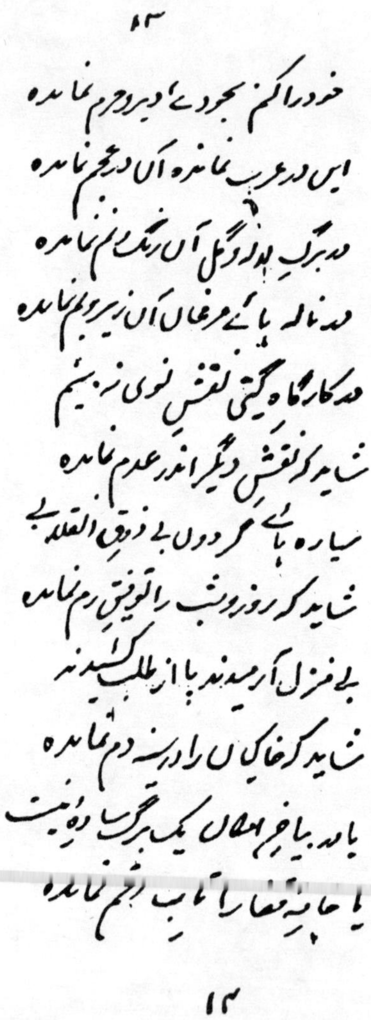
٤٣

خود را گم بجوئے دیر و حرم نماندہ
ایں در عرب نماندہ آں در عجم نماندہ
صد برگ بود از گل آں رنگ و نم نماندہ
صد نالہ ہائے مرغاں آں زیر و بم نماندہ
صد کارگاہِ گیتی نقشِ نوی نہ بینم
شاید کہ نقش دیگر اندر عدم نماندہ
سیارہ ہائے گردوں بے ذوقِ انقلابے
شاید کہ روز و شب را توفیقِ رم نماندہ
بے منزل آرمیدند پا از طلب کشیدند
شاید کہ خاکیاں را در سینہ دم نماندہ
باید بیا خرامان یک برگ سادہ ئی بیت
یا خامۂ قضا را تاب رقم نماندہ

١٤

Ms. of Poem 'The Pen of Fate' (in Farsi)

THE PEN OF FATE

I bow down before myself – there is no temple or Kaᶜbah left!
This one is missing in Arabia, that one in other lands.[1]

The petals of rose and tulip have lost their colour and moisture;
The laments of birds have lost their melody.[2]

In the workshop that is the world I see no new designs:
Pre-existence has, perhaps, run out of blueprints.[3]

The heavenly bodies no longer want to revolve:
Day and night are, perhaps, unable to move.

They have put up their feet before reaching their destination:
The earthlings have, perhaps, no breath left in their chests.

Either the Register of Possibles has no blank pages left
Or the Pen of Fate has grown too tired to write.[4]

ZA 423 [533]

[1]*I bow . . . lands:* Iqbal means that worship in temples and mosques has become so formalistic that they no longer deserve to be called by their names. True and sincere devotees therefore have no option but to treat themselves as the object of veneration, since they are a much more genuine embodiment of the purity and holiness customarily associated with places of worship. The word used for 'other lands' in the original is *ᶜAjam,* literally places other than Arabia – more precisely Persia. The phrase 'ᶜArab and ᶜAjam', when used in a context like the present, stands for the whole world.

[2]*The petals . . . melody:* If the world is like a garden, then the flowers of this garden have lost the beauty they once had, and bird-song has lost its melodious quality.

[3]*In the workshop . . . blueprints:* Plans conceived by God in pre-existence are executed in this world. If nothing new is happening in this world, it can only mean that nothing new is being planned in pre-existence. The word used for 'pre-existence' is *ᶜadam,* literally 'non-existence'. Cf. the final couplet.

[4]*the Register of Possibles:* The *bayad-i imkan* is the heavenly register in which God lists everything which is possible and will later become reality in the world. The couplet means that existence is now dull and monotonous because nothing new is being created. Cf. the third couplet.

VISION OF A NEW WORLD

There is a world still lost[1] in our hearts,
A world that still waits for the call of 'Rise!'[2]
A world without distinctions of blood and colour,
Where evening shines brighter
Than morning in the West;[3]
A world purged of sultan and slave,[4]
Boundless as a believer's heart;[5]
A glorious world, which had its seed cast
Into ᶜUmar's soul by a single holy look;[6]
An eternal world, but one whose events are always new,
Ever new the fruit[7] of its master principles;[8]
Within, it is not afflicted with change,
But outward change is occurring every moment.[9]
See, that world is inside you![10]
I will tell you what its master principles are . . .[11]

JN 539-40 [655]

[1]*still lost:* The world is 'lost' in the sense of the phrase 'lost treasure'. The adverb 'still' (*hanuz*, 'even now') is full of meaning. As we learn in the next few lines, the ideal world to which Iqbal alludes came into existence in the time of the second caliph, ᶜUmar. This being so, 'still' can only mean that that world ceased to exist long ago and has to be rediscovered. Iqbal's view of the rapid early expansion of Islam was somewhat different from the one usually held. He believed that the very rapidity of the great early Muslim conquests had made the construction of a model Islamic society on solid foundations impossible. In other words, what was gained in breadth was lost in depth. Since this happened so long ago, the ideal has remained unrealised for a long time.

[2]*A world . . . 'Rise!'* A world waiting for someone with the power to raise it from the dead – someone like Jesus, who brought the dead back to life by saying 'Rise!' (*qum*).

[3]*Where . . . West:* Iqbal was critical of the phenomenon of racism in the West, and the world envisaged by him was egalitarian in the truest sense. 'Where evening shines brighter than morning in the West' means: Even at its most ordinary ('evening') this new world will surpass the West at its most impressive ('morning').

[4]*A world purged . . . slave:* That is, where the unjust division of humankind into masters and slaves will be abolished. The thought expressed here is not to be dismissed as poetic fancy. Iqbal regarded kingship as the bane of historical Islamic civilisation, and his wish for a world without sultans or slaves is a powerful – and painful – reminder of the havoc wrought by the dominant

monarchical tradition in Islamic history. Note Iqbal's use of the strong word 'purged' (original: *pak*).

[5]*Boundless . . . heart:* It is said that the universe, though immeasurable, is still too small to accommodate God, but the believer's heart is large enough to house Him.

[6]*A glorious . . . look:* Looking for precedents for this ideal world, Iqbal settles on the era of the second caliph, ᶜUmar, who pioneered the establishment of major military, financial and social institutions in Islam, and is commonly regarded as the architect of the first great Islamic state. But it was the training he received from the Prophet Muhammad that enabled him to carry out his role and mission in Islamic history; it was the impact of the Prophet's look – Iqbal calls it a single look (*yak nazar*) – that transformed ᶜUmar, giving him the vision and energy that made the first great blossoming of Islamic civilisation possible.

[7]*fruit:* The original *barg-o-bar* means literally 'leaves and fruit'.

[8]*master principles:* The word used in the original is *muhkamat* (literally 'those made firm'), from Qur'an 3:7.

[9]*An eternal world . . . every moment:* This is possibly the most concise statement of one of the principal theses of Iqbal's philosophy. In his view, a nation's survival and progress depend on its ability to achieve a balance between change and constancy. Digging into the Islamic tradition for concepts to give structure to his argument, Iqbal comes up with *zahir* (exterior) and *batin* (interior). If a nation succeeds in developing an infrastructure of principles (let us call this its *batin*) with perennial validity, and then in every age builds new institutions (let us call them its *zahir*) that are organically derived from that *batin* and effectively meet the particular needs and challenges of the age in question, then that nation, according to Iqbal, has ensured its survival and is on the road to progress.

[10]*See . . . . you!* Note the envelope structure of the poem, which began with 'There is a world still lost in our hearts', and ends with a similar thought.

[11]In the several pages that follow in *Payam-i Mashriq*, Jamal ad-Din al-Afghani dwells on the *muhkamat* he has already referred to. That these, according to Iqbal, are derived from the Qur'an is borne out by the fact that the whole of Afghani's speech after these prefatory remarks is entitled *Muhkamat-i ᶜAlam-i Qur'ani* ('The Master Principles of the Qur'anic World'). The four sections into which the treatment is divided are entitled: 'Adam's Caliphate'; 'The Rule of God'; 'The Land Belongs to God' (a reference to such Qur'anic verses as 7:128); and 'Wisdom is a Great Good' (a reference to Qur'an 2:269).

12

QUATRAINS

In Persian and Urdu the quatrain, a poem of four lines, can be a *ruba'i* (usually with the rhyme scheme *aaba*) or a *qit'ah* (usually *abab*). The distinction is not entirely free of controversy; depending on whether the word 'quatrain' is used in the sense of *ruba'i* or *qit'ah*, or in both senses, the number of quatrains in Iqbal would vary. For our purposes a quatrain is either a *ruba'i* or a four-line piece which, even without the rhyme scheme of a *ruba'i*, occurs in Iqbal's works intermixed with *ruba'is*. According to this definition, there are 609 quatrains in Iqbal's poetical works. Of these 557 are in Persian (*Payam-i Mashriq*: 163; *Armaghan-i Hijaz*: 394) and 52 in Urdu (*Bal-i Jibril*: 39; *Armaghan-i Hijaz*: 13). The sheer number indicates the importance Iqbal attached to the quatrain as a vehicle for his thought. This is further underscored when we note that most of the quatrains are in Persian, Iqbal's preferred language for the expression of his mature thought. The quatrains treat many of the principal themes of Iqbal's poetry, and as such are a kaleidoscope of his thought and a good introduction to many of the themes of his poetry.

In this chapter the quatrains are cited by (1) the abbreviated title of the work in which they appear; (2) the page number, although, as in the other chapters, this belongs to the Persian or Urdu *Kulliyyat* volume rather than to an individual work in either volume; and (3) their number on the page cited (the first *complete* quatrain on a page is counted as the first), irrespective of whether they are numbered in the original work itself or not. Again, as in the other chapters, the Iqbal Academy edition is cited first, and is followed by the Sheikh Ghulam Ali edition, in square brackets. Thus *PM* 228:5 [231:2] means that the quatrain occurs in *Payam-i Mashriq*, is to be found on page 228 of the Iqbal Academy *Kulliyyat-i Iqbal – Farsi* edition, and is no. 5 on that page; and on page 231 of the Sheikh Ghulam Ali *Kulliyyat-i Iqbal – Farsi* edition, where it is quatrain no. 2.

EXISTENCE

According to Iqbal, existence is a dynamic unity. It is a unity because all things owe their existence to the One God; and it is dynamic because it constantly manifests itself in newer forms. The principle underlying this dynamic unity is love, for which Iqbal uses the word *ʿishq*. For him, *ʿishq*, (we are not concerned here with the other senses in which he uses the word) produces the spring breeze, causes the buds to flower, gives the tulip its colour, guides the fish through the sea, and fills human beings with boundless ambition; it can even be seen as pumping blood into the veins of the 'body' of this terrestrial world if one could only dissect that body. Is this poetic imagination run wild or does the thought have some substance? Iqbal seems to be dealing with the question of appearance and reality. He suggests that normally the distinctions made between the material and the abstract, the physical and the spiritual are constructs that may make it easy for us to understand the phenomenal world and deal with it, but also prevent us from having a full view of reality, which is made possible only if these distinctions, or rather barriers, are abolished. In a well-known line Iqbal says that if the heart of an atom were dissected, the blood of the sun would drip from that heart (*BD* 302 [271]). It is only through intuition that one can see the bonds of unity in the universe, but for Iqbal intuition is a philosophical rather than a mystical concept; what he has in mind is not the panthesitic monism which a Sufi experiences in a state of ecstasy, but the existential unity which a thinker is able to establish cognitively, seeing through the artificial walls separating one existent or species from another. In this view existential unity, since it ultimately derives from God, the creator of all, no longer remains value-neutral but becomes a positive good.

But while subscribing on a philosophical level to the notion of existential unity, Iqbal is not oblivious (as a pantheistic Sufi would be) of the imperfections, shortcomings, and evil and injustice of the everyday world, about all of which he has some hard things to say. He is also unhappy that the precious and beautiful things of this world do not last very long. So is this the best of all possible worlds? The question takes us back to the poems of the first chapter, which expressed similar concerns.

DYNAMIC UNITY

His glory is seen in garden and jungle;
The cup of the rose glows with His wine.
There is no one whom He consigns to everlasting darkness –
From His mark a lamp is lit in every heart.[1]

PM 228:5 [231:2]

[1] *From His . . . heart:* God has put His mark in every heart, and from this mark is lit a lamp, which dispels any darkness that might surround that heart.

What joy comes with existence, dear Lord!
The heart of every atom yearns for life:
As the rose-bud cracks open the branch,
It smiles with the love of life!

PM 211:1 [201:3]

Our world, a piece of work not yet finished,
Is hostage to the alteration of day and night;
The file of fate will rub it smooth –
This clay sculpture is still being made.[1]

PM 227:2 [228:3]

[1] *The file . . . made:* Nature is ever at work, giving rise to new possibilities.

EVIL, SUFFERING AND INJUSTICE

Who created the world out of his own self?
Whose unveiled glory does its beauty represent?
You say to me, 'Beware of Satan!'
But tell me: Who nurtured him?[1]

AHF 772:1 [888:3]

[1] *You say . . . him?* These lines raise the issue of the existence of evil. God commands human beings to be on their guard against Satan, but is it not true that God Himself created and nurtured Satan?

This is a world which is made even darker by the sun,
Its right is wrong all through.

I do not know for how long You will use
Adam's blood to give it colour and glow![1]

AHF 773:4 [891:3]

[1] *This is . . . glow!* This world is full of evil, and any beauty it might possess is tainted because it has been achieved at the cost of human suffering. How long will God allow this state of affairs to continue?

A hungry disciple said to his master:
'God does not know of our state:
He is closer to us than our jugular veins,[2]
But not as close as our bellies'.
AHF 778:1 [899:1]

[1] *He is . . . veins:* A reference to Qur'an 50:16: 'And We are closer to him [man] than his jugular vein.'

TRANSIENCE OF THE WORTHY AND THE BEAUTIFUL

The nightingale said to the gardener at dawn:
'Only the tree of sorrow can take root in this soil:
The wild thorn reaches a ripe age,
But the rose dies when it is still young'.

PM 208:5 [198:1]

On the Day of Resurrection the Brahmin said to God:
'The light of life was like a brilliant spark;
But, if you don't mind, I will say this to you:
The idol lasted longer than man'

PM 210:2 [200:2]

THE HUMAN BEING

Human beings have an affinity with God, and may be said to contain the divine spark. However, the distinction between God the Creator and human beings, His creation, is firmly established in Iqbal, who emphasises the importance of the human being's role as the servant-worshipper of God. A human being's highest goal should be to become not God (*khuda'i*) but the perfect servant-worshipper (*bandagi*).

Human beings are composed of *gil*, *khirad* and *dil*. *Gil* (literally 'clay') is the physical element in their composition; *khirad* (literally 'reason'; Iqbal frequently uses *'aql* as its synonym) is the intellectual element; and *dil* (literally 'heart') is the spiritual-intuitive element. *Khirad* raises human beings above animals, but it is *dil* that is their truly distinctive characteristic; *khirad* is indispensable, but it should ideally be subservient to *dil*. Iqbal seems to be critical of the definition of the human being as a rational animal, which he would regard as invalid or at least inadequate. Since human beings are the finest of all creation's products, their *dil* is the most highly prized thing in the world; according to Iqbal (*PM* 208:4 [197:3]), *jahan musht-i gil-o-dil hasil-i u'st*, 'The world is a handful of dust, and the heart is its choicest product'. There is indeed a sense in which the heart can be said to be vaster than the world itself and even to include the world (*PM* 220:4 [217:3]).

Although it is a mystery how *dil* could be housed in *gil*, the physical body is nevertheless essential to human existence; it gives a more forceful expression to human intellectual and spiritual potentialities (to use one of Iqbal's images, the body is a scabbard that both protects and whets the sword of *dil*). Being the unique essence of the human being, *dil* is not subject to the laws governing the body, it does not die with the body and is the cause of all exciting activity in this world. *Dil*, possession of which puts human beings above the angels, remains *dil* only for as long as it is kept alive and vibrant.

Human beings are, as proposed above, servant-worshippers of God. They are, however, creative beings; in a sense they may be called co-workers of God and as such superior to the rest of creation – and hence the measure of all things. But Iqbal calls human beings the measure of all things not in the sense in which the Greek Sophists called them that, but in the sense that they must not allow their worth to be reckoned in terms of things which themselves are subject to evaluation by them – which would be a great irony.

Some ironies of human life are quite real, however. For one thing, there is a marked incompatibility between the ambitious spirit and the weak flesh. For another, while human beings have conquered nature, they still have very little insight into their own selves. Still, they must continue to strive for perfection and pursue higher and nobler goals.

AFFINITY WITH GOD

Your plectrum fills the instrument of the soul with tunes.[1]
How can You be in the soul and outside it as well?[2]
Why should I worry? With Yọu, I am aflame;[3] without You, I die.
But my Unique One, how do You manage without me?[4]

PM 222:4 [221:1]

[1]*Your plectrum . . . tunes:* You (God) enable the soul to sing its song. In other words, the activity of the heart and mind is due to God.

[2]*How can . . . as well?* If you produce the song the soul sings, then in a sense You are inside the soul. But You are also outside it? How can You be both at the same time?

[3]*With You, I am aflame:* I have life on account of You.

[4]*But my . . . me?* Although You are unique and as such do not need anyone else to complete Your being, I would like to know how You are without me. The allusion is to Adam's departure from paradise. Adam cannot live without God, but how is God faring without Adam? The expected answer is that God misses Adam and wants him to return.

BEING GOD AND BEING A SERVANT OF GOD

To be God is to have charge of land and sea;[1]
Being God is nothing but a headache![2]
But being a servant of God? God forbid!
That is no headache – it is a heartache![3]

BJ 413:2 [380:2]

[1]*land and sea:* i.e. the whole world. The original, *khushk-o-tar,* literally means 'dry and wet'.

[2]*Being God . . . headache!* Because of the huge responsibility of administering this world (see line 1).

[3]*heartache!* Iqbal uses the word in a positive sense – *sweet* heartache. Being a servant of God is a heartache in the sense that one longs for the fulfilment of one's desires and dreams, and also in the sense that one feels for one's fellow human beings and tries to alleviate their suffering. The perfection of a human being thus consists not in becoming God but in becoming truly human.

REASON AND HEART

Reason makes the traveller sharp-sighted.[1]
What is reason? It is a lamp that lights up our path.
The commotion raging inside the house –
What does the traveller's lamp know of it![2]

BJ 410:4 [377:4]

[1]*Reason . . . sharp-sighted:* The traveller is the human being passing through this transient, inn-like world.

[2]*What does . . . it!* Reason has no knowledge of what occurs in the realm of the heart.

He could not have tested the strength of his *khudi*
Or freed his own hands and feet from chains;
Reason would have been chains to man,
If he had not had a heart within him.

AHF 848:1 [1000:2]

My heart! My heart! My heart!
My ocean, my boat, my shore![1]
Did you fall like dew on my dusty being,
Or did you sprout like a bud out of my soil?[2]

PM 224:1 [223:2]

[1]*My heart! . . . my shore!* I am a traveller in this world, and you, my heart, are everything to me – the ocean on which I travel, the boat in which I sail, and the shore on which I set foot (incidentally, the three occurrences of 'My heart!' in the first line correspond each to the ocean, the boat and the shore in the second). The lines can be understood as a celebration of a life lived in accordance with the dictates of the heart as opposed to one lived mechanically ('heartlessly') – the heart being the most prized possession of human beings.

[2]*Did you fall . . . soil?* Are you a gift from the heavens ('like dew') or are you the result of a process of growth and evolution that occured in my own being.

Iqbal means to say that it is hard to explain how a non-earthly element (heart) became part of an earthly creature. The question asked by him is analogous to one that has been raised in philosophy: is the so-called mind distinct from matter or only a developed form of it?

A CREATIVE BEING

To the voice of love Adam is music;[1]
He reveals secrets, but he is a secret himself.
God created the world, but Adam made it better –
Adam, perhaps, is God's co-worker.

PM 209:2 [198:3]

[1]*music:* Literally 'musical instrument'. Like accompanying music, the human being sets off the voice of love. Love (*ʿishq*) here stands for devotion and commitment to noble ideals, pursuit of which, according to Iqbal, became possible only with the birth of the human being.

Just for once weigh up gain against loss:[1]
Make this world eternal like paradise.
Can You not see all that we, creatures of dust,
Have done to adorn this earth?[2]

AHF 778:4 [900:1]

[1]*Just . . . loss:* Iqbal wants God to make a reappraisal: must Adam remain under a curse for disobeying God during his stay in heaven, or should he be rewarded for making this earthly world a beautiful place to live in? What was gained by expelling man from heaven – and what was lost?

[2]*Make this world. . . earth?* Human beings have done so much to adorn this world that they have no need to go back to the paradise from which their first ancestors were expelled. This world, however, is not eternal, and God, seeing the role of human beings in turning it into a beautiful place, should be appreciative: He should reward them by making this world eternal – after which, of course, human beings will have a paradise away from paradise.

THE HUMAN BEING AS THE MEASURE OF ALL THINGS

If you were merely to glance at a piece of rock,
It would turn into a jewel if you so desired.
Slave of gold, don't measure yourself by gold –
It was your glance that turned it into gold.

PM 219:4 [216:1]

THE CALCULATING HUMAN BEING

Make me fill this world with commotion,[1]
And completely change the earth and the sky.
Raise a new Adam from our dust,
And kill this slave of profit and loss.[2]

AHF 773:3 [891:2]

[1]*Make . . . commotion:* The world needs to be roused from its torpor by means of the commotion that rages in my soul.

[2]*Raise a new. . . loss:* Create a new Adam and kill the present Adam, who is unable to rise above the petty considerations of monetary profit and loss.

THE QUEST ETERNAL

I do not seek the beginning or the end;
I am full of mystery and seek the realm of mysteries.
Even if the face of truth were unveiled,
I would still seek the same 'perhaps' and 'maybe'.[1]

PM 209:3 [199:1]

[1]*Even if . . . 'maybe'*: 'Perhaps' and 'maybe' stand for uncertainty and doubt – which motivate one to investigate and discover. The lines mean that the quest for truth is more exciting than its attainment.

I was raised long ago in this earthly place,
But I do not care for my home.[1]
I owe my very life to its bountiful moisture,[2]
But the earth is not my sky.[3]

AHF 861:3 [1018:2]

[1]*But I . . . home:* I do not wish to remain attached to the earth, my home, for I set my goals high (see the last line).

[2]*I owe . . . moisture:* The poet compares himself to a plant or tree that owes its existence to the moisture in the soil; 'its' refers to the 'earthly place' of the first line.

[3]*But . . . sky:* I do not regard it as my 'ceiling'.

IRONIES OF HUMAN LIFE

Inside me is such a play of ideas – what does this mean?
Outside me are all these mysteries – what does this mean?
Say, you who are wise and have a subtle mind:
The body lies still, but the soul stirs – what does this mean?[1]

PM 231:4 [236:1]

[1]The quatrain raises the issue of the sharp dichotomy between the outer and inner aspects of human existence – that is, between the life of the body and the life of the heart or soul.

The philosophers have broken a hundred idols,
But they are still in the Somnat of 'was' and 'is'.[1]
How can they ensnare the angels and God? –
They have not yet tied Adam to their saddle-straps! [2]

PM 230:5 [234:3]

[1]*Somnat of 'was' and 'is':* Somnat is a famous Hindu temple in Gujerat, India; 'was' and 'is' represent time as divided into the narrow categories of past and present. To remain a prisoner of such categories and fail to see truth in its timeless aspect is like idol-worshipping – and this is the failure of the philosophers: for all their intellectual prowess, they have not learned to think *sub specie aeternitatis* (under the aspect of eternity). They are thus no better than those who worship idols in Somnat or other temples.

[2]*How can . . . saddle-straps!* How can the philosophers, the would-be hunters riding out in the field of thought, solve the mystery surrounding God and angels when they have not yet solved the mystery of Adam? The image in the last line is of a hunter fastening the game he has killed to the saddle-strap of his horse.

This Adam – is he the sovereign of land and sea?
What can I say about such an incompetent being!
He is not able to see anything – himself, God, or the world!
Is this the masterpiece of Your art?

BJ 413:3 [380:3]

KHUDI

The complex concept of *khudi* (literally 'selfhood') has an important place in Iqbal's work (see introduction to Chapter 10). As one's essential and authentic potential, *khudi* seeks actualisation. *Khudi* is positive by nature, and cultivation of it brings good, just as smothering it leads to harm. Self-understanding, self-growth and self-expression are the goals of *khudi*; self-esteem, self-reliance and independence of mind make up its ethos; and dynamism, creativity and adventure are its modes of operation. But ultimately human *khudi* has an affinity with the Divine Being, and an understanding of the one gives one an insight into the other (in the second quatrain of this section – and implicitly in the first too – Iqbal makes punning use of the words *khudi* and *khuda*, the latter being the Persian for 'God'). In the subsection 'Modes of Khudi: Dynamism, Creativity and Adventure' the first two quatrains are to be read together.

KHUDI AND GOD

God is the ground of *khudi*'s existence
Khudi's own manifestation is due to God's.
Where would this luminous pearl have been
Had no ocean existed?[1]

AHF 850:2 [1003:3]

[1] *Where would . . . existed?* Iqbal likens human *khudi* to a pearl and God to an ocean.

On my behalf tell the pure-hearted Sufis –
Those seekers after God and possessors of the truth:
I would humbly serve that resolute self-worshipper[1]
Who sees God in the light of his own *khudi*.'[2]

PM 232:4 [237:3]

[1] *I would . . . self-worshipper: Ghulam-i himmat-i an khud-parastam* literally translates: 'I am a servant of the resolution of that self-worshipper'. *Himmat* ('resolution'; Arabic *himmah*) is a Sufi term, implying total commitment to the goal of achieving spiritual perfection and closeness to God. 'Self-worshipper' in this context is one who has self-esteem and self-confidence – that is, one who has kept his *khudi* intact.

[2]*Who sees . . . khudi:* According to Iqbal, the highest state of *khudi* is that in which, having achieved complete self-fulfillment, one subjects one's *khudi* to the commandments of God or, as this quatrain puts it, sees God in the light of one's *khudi*.

GOALS OF *KHUDI*: SELF-UNDERSTANDING, SELF-GROWTH AND SELF-EXPRESSION

You went to Sinai, begging to have a view;
Your soul is a stranger to itself.[1]
Set out in search of man;
God Himself is searching for him.

PM 216:2 [210:2]

[1]*You went . . . itself:* Iqbal says that one's attention should be focused on one's own *khudi* since there is no need to beg others for enlightenment – even if that means begging God for a view. The reference is to Qur'an 7:143, which reports Moses as expressing his wish to see God with his own eyes.

You follow a path into the very heart of stars,[1]
But you do not know your own self.
Just for once look at your self like a seed,
So that you will grow out of the earth like a tree.[2]

PM 211:5 [203:1].

[1]*You follow . . . stars:* You probe into stars and discover their secrets.
[2]*Just for once . . . tree:* The secret of human existence lies within the human self. Cf. Chapter 4, 'The Story of Adam'.

ETHOS OF *KHUDI*: SELF-ESTEEM, SELF-RELIANCE AND INDEPENDENCE OF MIND

Carve out your path with your own pick-axe;
It is a torment to take the path of others.
If what you can do is unique,
It will deserve a reward even if it is a sin.

PM 227:4 [229:2]

In the midst of water and earth I sat alone,[1]
And turned away from Plato and Farabi.[2]
I did not beg anyone else for sight –
I saw the world with my eyes alone.

PM 228:2 [230:2]

[1]*In the midst . . . alone:* 'Water and earth' (*ab-o-gil*) stands for the human body, which is made up of the two elements. The line means: I transcended my physical limitations and came into contact with my essential self. The Persian phrase, if interpreted as *jahan-i ab-o-gil,* 'the world made of water and earth', would give the same meaning (for the human frame is a microcosm – made of water and earth), but it may also mean the universe, in which case the poet would be saying that he withdrew from the physical world so as to tap into and explore his own self.

[2]*And turned away . . . Farabi:* His choice of these two names enables Iqbal to score a double hit: (1) to follow the Greek philosopher thinker Plato (d. 347 BC) or the Muslim thinker Farabi (tenth century) would be to follow the path of others; (2) Farabi himself followed Plato, writing a book in the style of the *Republic,* which relied heavily on it for content and perspective, and so to follow Farabi would be to commit a compound sin.

How long, my heart, will you be as foolish as the moth?
How long will you be unlike a man's heart?
Just for once let your own fire consume you –
How long will you fly round the fire of others?

PM 209:4 [199:2]

MODES OF *KHUDI*: DYNAMISM, CREATIVITY, AND ADVENTURE

A crocodile spoke aptly to its youngster:
'In our creed the shore is a forbidden place!
Avoid it but let the wave break upon you –
The whole ocean is our home!

'You are not in the ocean, the ocean is in your arms:
To plunge into the storm – that is to be your true self!
If its storms should cease just for a moment,
The same ocean will be your ruin!'

AHF 836:2-3 [985:2-3]

Alexander gave Khizr some good advice:[1]
'Be part of the commotion of land and sea.
You are watching this battle from the side of the field;
Go and die in action, and then you will be truly immortal.'[2]

PM 213:4 [206:1]

[1] *Alexander . . . advice:* Khizr (the alternative pronunciation, 'Khizar', is used in the original; Arabic: Khidr), a legendary figure who is the 'patron saint' of the waters. He is said to have found the fountain of life and drunk from it. He is also said to have guided Alexander to the fountain, although Alexander did not drink from it. As Alexander's guide, Khizr is superior to him, but he is represented here as receiving advice from him – a reversal of roles.
[2] *'Be part . . . immortal':* Alexander explains what true immortality is: it is not living for ever in temporal terms, but living an active, dynamic life, which will enable one to live on even after physical death.

Don't arrange a party on the shore,
For there the song of life is gentle and soft.
Roll with the ocean and contend with its waves:
Struggle and combat give eternal life.

PM 219:1 [215:1]

I have heard that in pre-existence the moth said:[1]
'Grant me just a moment's radiance in my life.
You may scatter my ashes at dawn,
But grant me one night of passion and fire'.[2]

PM 211:2 [202:1]

[1] *I have . . . said:* The moth, which flies round the light until it dies, lives a short but passionate life (see following lines). God must have granted it its wish for such a life while it was still in pre-existence. In other words, the moth by nature prefers such a life to one that is long but dull. Iqbal obviously approves.
[2] *But grant . . . fire:* That is, allow me to fly round the burning lamp all night in love and devotion.

To a fearless heart a lion is a sheep;
To a timid heart a deer is a tiger.
If you have no fear, the ocean is a desert;
If you are fearful, there is a crocodile in every wave.

PM 226:2 [227:1]

What fruit will the bough of my hope bear –
What do I know of your destiny?[1]
The rose-bud needs to open today –
Why wait for tomorrow's morning breeze?[2]

AHU 729:1 [671:1]

[1] *What fruit . . . destiny?* The poet hopes that the Muslim community (represented by the person being addressed) will have a bright future, but has no way of telling whether this will actually happen. In these two lines the poet is represented as responding to an unexpressed question: the addressee wishes to know whether he will succeed in life (what his 'destiny' is), and whether he will be able to fulfill the expectations the poet has of him (whether the poet's 'bough of hope' will bear fruit).

[2] *The rose-bud . . . breeze?* Having expressed ignorance of what the future holds for the addressee, the poet suggests to him that one has charge of one's destiny, and that one will succeed by leading an active, purposeful life and becoming self-reliant in the present rather than by idly waiting for help from external sources ('tomorrow's morning breeze').

This revolution of time is eternal;
Only you are real, the rest is nothing but tales and legends.
No one has ever seen yesterday or tomorrow:
Today is the only time that is yours![1]

BJ 414:3 [381:3]

[1] *No one . . . yours!* As Iqbal says in more than one place, a nation that glories in its past, forgetting to act in the present, deludes itself, and a nation that does not act in the present has no right to claim the future as its own.

FREEDOM AND DETERMINISM AND THE PHILOSOPHY OF HISTORY

In Iqbal the two subjects are closely related. Even when he appears to be discussing the issue of freedom and determinism for the individual, it is usually society he has in mind, and the forces that influence the rise and fall of nations make up the context. At times Iqbal acknowledges the role of fate in determining the course of history, but at other times he avoids making an explicit statement, saying only that the 'drama' of human life has not yet come to an end, and one cannot therefore put forward a final opinion on the subject. But as a rule Iqbal holds that nations control their own destinies and deserve credit or blame according to their success or failure in the world. Iqbal is influenced by Ibn Khaldun's philosophy of history: the forces that generate a new civilisation arise from an environment that sets a premium on toughness, promotes self-pride and self-reliance, and engenders a spirit of adventure and self-sacrifice. In the life of a nation individuals are important but not indispensable.

Why is there no storm in your sea?[1]
Why is your *khudi* not Muslim?[2]
It is pointless to complain of God's decree –
Why are *you* not God's decree?

AHU 734:2 [674:3]

[1] *sea:* Although in Urdu the word *darya* ordinarily means river, 'sea' appears to be more appropriate here.
[2] *Why is there . . . Muslim?* Just as a sea should not be without a storm, so one's life should not lack dynamism. A Muslim (literally 'one who submits [to God]') whose *khudi* is also Muslim is expected to live a life full of action.

My entire being is a meaning sealed,
I cannot abide the looks of word-spinners.[1]
I cannot be called free – or pre-determined –
Because I am living clay, and for ever changing![2]

PM 219:2 [215:2]

[1] *word-spinners:* Those who deal in words, and shut their eyes to meaning. In this context (see last two lines), the word-spinners are those who split hairs while discussing the issue of freedom and determinism, but take a partial view of matter and are therefore misguided.

[1] *I cannot be . . . changing!* The whole discussion of free will and determinism is irrelevant since human life is too dynamic to be interpreted in terms of such limited categories of thought.

In Rome an old monk said to me:
'I have a piece of wisdom, and I give it to you:
Every nation causes its own downfall –
You were destroyed by fate, we by our strategy.'[1]

AHF 851:3 [1005/2]

[1] *You . . . strategy:* That is, the Muslim world disintegrated because of the Muslims' fatalism, while the Roman Empire was reduced to ruin by the very strategies used to preserve it.

The rumbling thunder of tomorrow's dawn belongs
Only to those nights which are lit up by Sinai's epiphanies.[1]
The winds of the wild toughen the body and the soul –
It is from deserts and mountains that nations arise.

AHF 824:4 [968:1]

[1] *The rumbling . . . epiphanies:* Alluding to the life of the Israelites in the desert after their exodus from Egypt, Iqbal says that glory is won only through action and struggle: only those nations may expect to see their 'night' (adversity) followed by 'morning' (prosperity) which have a clear sense of purpose. 'Sinai's epiphanies' refers to God's manifestation of Himself on Mount Sinai (see Qur'an 7:143).

God gives that nation sovereignty
Which inscribes its fate with its own hand;
He will have nothing to do with the nation
Whose peasants till the land for others.

AHF 813:3 [950:3]

Alexander is gone, with his sword and banner,
The revenue he collected, and his treasures from mines and oceans.
You must believe that nations are more lasting than kings:
Don't you see that Iran survives, but not Jamshed?[1]

PM 234:1 [240:1]

[1] *Jamshed:* A legendary king of ancient Persia.

CRITICISM OF THE MODERN AGE

The modern age is notable for its loss of faith (faith in the twin senses of religion or God-consciousness and certitude or conviction). Despite its claim to bestow freedom and dignity on human beings, it has actually put them in chains.

What is this age, which religion laments?
Its freedom comes with a thousand chains.
It has robbed man's face of brightness and moisture.[1]
The picture its Bihzad[2] has made is fake.

AHF 830:4 [977:1]

[1]*It has . . . moisture:* It has robbed human beings of their dignity and honour.
[2]*Bihzad:* One of the greatest painters of Iran (d. after 1514). The choice of Bihzad is significant, since he broke with tradition and popularised a new style of painting. Modernity, likewise, has broken with tradition – but the new style of life and culture introduced by its Bihzad has serious shortcomings.

Faith, like Abraham, sits down in the fire;[1]
To have faith is to be drawn into God and to be oneself.[2]
Listen, you captive of modern civilisation,
To lack faith is worse than slavery!

BJ 406:4 [373:4]

[1]*Faith, like . . . fire:* A reference to Qur'an 21:68-71, according to which Abraham was thrown into a fire by his disbelieving people, but God came to his rescue, commanding the fire to 'become cool' for him. The line means that true faith or conviction (the word used in the original is *yaqin*) would not shrink from being put to the test.
[2]*To have faith . . . oneself:* It is being suggested that there is no contradiction between 'being drawn into God' and 'being oneself', for affirmation of one's selfhood (*khudi*) will lead one to affirmation of God, and *vice versa* (see section on *Khudi*, above).

The Muslim combined kingship with poverty,[1]
The eternal with the transient.[2]
But God save us from the present age,
Which combines kingship with devilship!

AHF 831:2 [978:1]

[1]*The Muslim . . . poverty:* The Prophet, who became the ruler of Arabia, said that poverty was his pride (*al-faqru fakhri*), and some of the best rulers of Islam upheld that ideal. 'Poverty' here means lack of attachment to the world and worldly goods (see Chapter 1, 'Do One of the Two!', n. 6).

[2]*The eternal . . . transient:* Muslims captured the universal vision of their religion in local contexts.

MUSLIMS

Iqbal holds Muslims responsible for their abject state in the world. They are disunited and prone to fight among themselves; they lead aimless lives with no higher objectives to pursue; they are apathetic towards their religion and tradition; and in general they have servile habits and attitudes. Their institutions – religious, political, educational, and cultural – have also become decadent. Muslims do not have leaders who would bring them out of this morass, and the leaders they do have hardly deserve the title. In one of the quatrains that follow, Iqbal advises Muslim women to 'veil' themselves from the modern age and concentrate on raising a better generation.

THEIR SORRY STATE: SCHISM AND PURPOSELESSNESS

Muslims are at war with one another –
And in their hearts they harbour only schism;[1]
They cry out if someone else pulls a brick
Out of the mosque which they themselves shun.[2]

AHF 792:5 [921:1]

[1]*And in . . . schism:* Iqbal makes punning use of the Persian word for 'schism', *du'i,* which means both 'duality' and 'duplicity'. As monotheists, Muslims must not entertain any notion of duality, and their life must not be marked by duplicity if they claim to be true believers. Iqbal is saying that the internal schism of Muslims contravenes the very doctrine they hold: as believers in one God, they should be one community. The line may also be translated: 'In their hearts they harbour only duality.'
[2]*They cry out . . . shun:* That is, their attachment to their religion is almost entirely sentimental.

One night I burst into tears before God –
'Why are Muslims in such a wretched state?'
There came a voice, 'Don't you know that this nation
Has a heart, but nothing to set its heart on?'[1]

AHF 794:1 [923:1]

[1]*nothing to set its heart on:* No noble objectives to pursue.

His pure blood has lost its brilliance,
And tulips no longer grow in his wasteland.
His scabbard is empty, just like his purse,[1]
And his Book is in the vault of a house in ruins.[2]

AHF 789:1 [914:3]

[1]*His scabbard . . . purse:* Muslims have neither military nor economic power.
[2]*And his . . . ruins:* Muslims have forgotten the Qur'an, which they have consigned to a vault in their house – the house itself being in ruins.

THE MULLA, THE SUFI AND
THE WESTERNISED MUSLIM

My greetings to the Mulla and the Sufi,
For they delivered God's message to us!
But their interpretation of it has left
God, Gabriel[1] and Muhammad astonished.

AHF 816-7: 5 [956:1]

[1]*Gabriel:* The angel who conveyed God's revelation to Muhammad.

Iqbal said to the *shaykh* of the Ka^cbah:[1]
'Who went to sleep under the very arch in the mosque?'
A voice sounded from the walls of the mosque:
'Who became lost in the idol-house of the West?'[2]

AHU 732:1 [673:1]

[1]*the shaykh of the Ka^cbah:* The phrase *shaykh-i haram* means literally 'chief of the Ka^cbah', i.e. the chief scholar or representative of Islam.
[2]The quatrain offers a balanced criticism of the attitudes of traditional and modernist Muslims. Iqbal, here representing the Westernised Muslims, criticises traditional Muslim authorities for going to sleep in the mosque – for confining themselves to ritual and prayer and failing to play a positive and effective role in a changed world. Before the *shaykh-i haram* can respond, a voice arises from the walls of the mosque and takes Iqbal to task for his failure to play *his* part: he has become too enamoured of Western culture and thought and, becoming lost in the idol-house of the West, has forgotten his own responsibilites towards the Muslim community.

You pay homage to Darius and Jamshed[1] –
But that is a disgrace to the Kaᶜbah!
Do not present petitions to the *Farangi*:
Tear this idol from the alcove of your heart![2]

AHF 863:3 [1021:3]

[1]*Darius and Jamshed:* Three kings of ancient Persia were named Darius, the most famous being Darius I (the Great), d. 486. Jamshed was a legendary ruler of ancient Persia.

[2]*Do not petition . . . heart!* Do not rely on Europe for help (*Farangi* is a generic name for Europeans), for that would be tantamount to worshipping Europe (the *Farangi* is called an idol that must be abandoned). Instead, become self-reliant.

MUSLIM INSTITUTIONS

The goblets at the *khanaqah*[1] contain no wine,
And in schools they are treading the beaten track;[2]
I left the gatherings of poets despondent:
The tunes of their flutes are stillborn.

AHF 793:3 [922:1]

[1]*khanaqah:* Sufi retreat or monastery.

[2]*And in schools . . . track:* The educational system has become outdated, and the schools and colleges are no longer producing creative minds or fresh thought.

I owe this reason-nurturing love[1] of mine
To the look of a mother with a pure heart.
School gives you neither eyes nor heart,
For school is no more than illusion and magic.[2]

AHF 829:4 [975:3]

[1]*reason-nurturing love:* To Iqbal, the ideal relation between emotion and reason is one of harmony and complementarity and not of conflict, a theme explored in Chapter 5 above. 'Reason-nurturing love' represents this ideal.

[2]The quatrain shows Iqbal's disillusionment with the Muslim educational system in India (and by extension in the greater Muslim world). The training children receive at home can, however, make a difference in their lives, as it did in Iqbal's (see Introduction).

Arabia, aglow with Muhammad's light,
Kindled the dead lamp of the East.
But then that Caliphate which had first taught
The believers how to rule went off-course.

AHF 827:1 [971:3]

DIAGNOSIS: LACK OF COMMITMENT AND LOSS OF *KHUDI*

They no longer have that passionate love –
Muslims are drained of blood.[1]
The rows are uneven, the hearts adrift, the prostration joyless[2] –
All this because the inner feeling is dead!

BJ 410:1 [377:1]

[1] *They . . . blood:* Muslims no longer feel the commitment to their religion they once had.

[1] *The rows . . . joyless:* Muslims' disunity and weak faith can be seen during prayer. As they line up in the mosque to pray, the rows they make are uneven (they are supposed to be even), their hearts lack the required concentration, and the prostration they perform lacks the element of joy.

The Muslim's physique is sturdy,
His bodily frame is in fine shape;
But the wise physician knows from the look in his eyes,
That his *khudi* is paralysed within him.

AHF 791:1[918.1]

THE CURE: UNITY THROUGH FAITH, REAWAKENING OF *KHUDI* AND BUILDING OF CHARACTER

We are not Afghans, Turks or Tartars:
Offspring of the garden, we grew from the same bough.
Distinctions of colour and scent are forbidden to us,
For we are products of a new spring.

PM 223:4 [222:3]

He who strikes his *khudi* with *La ilah*[1]
Produces a seeing eye from dead earth; [2]

Take hold of the hem of such a man,
For I have seen him lasso the sun and moon.[3]

AHF 813-4:5 [951:2]

[1]*He who . . . La ilah:* The believer who disciplines his *khudi* by subjecting it to the dictates of the Islamic confession of faith, *La ilaha illa llah* (of which *La ilah* is an abbreviation), 'There is no god but God'. See also next note.
[2]*Produces . . . earth:* Brings to life a dead body, which now possesses sight and other faculties. In other words, *khudi* fortified by belief in One God will equip one with insight.
[3]*Take hold . . . moon:* Such a person has risen to the highest level of perfection and should be held in great esteem.

Build, with your handful of dust,
A body stronger than a rock fortress,
and inside this body let there be a heart that feels sorrow –
Like a stream flowing by a mountain.[1]

PM 209:5 [199:3]

[1]In this quatrain Iqbal says that one needs to have a strong body in order to meet the challenges of life, and a feeling heart in order to appreciate life's delicate aspects. He expresses this idea by using a simile: the strong body is like a mountain whereas the feeling heart is like a stream flowing by it.

ADVICE TO MUSLIM WOMEN

The world owes its stability to mothers,
Their being is the repository of the possible.[1]
If a nation is ignorant of this truth,
Its system of life will not have a firm foundation.

AHF 829:3 [975:2]

[1]*Their being . . . possible:* The children they bear and bring up will help the world realise its potential, translating possibility into reality.

From our evening bring forth morning,
With the Qur'an call back[1] those with insight;
Your impassioned recitation, as you know well,
Changed the fate of ʿUmar completely![2]

AHF 830:3 [976:3]

[1]*Call back:* Or 'challenge'. See also next note.
[2]*Your . . . ᶜUmar completely!* ᶜUmar, Muhammad's Companion and second caliph of Islam, is reported to have embraced Islam after listening to his sister reciting the Qur'an. In the light of this historical incident, line 2 would mean: renew the Muslims's faith and transform them by means of the Qur'an, just as ᶜUmar's sister transformed him with her Qur'an recitation.

Heed the counsel of a *dervish*[1]
And even if a thousand nations perish, you will not die.
Be a Fatimah and hide from this age,
So that you may cradle a Husayn in your arms.[2]

AHF 830:2 [976:2]

[1]*the counsel of a dervish:* A *dervish* is one who has risen above the world, is apparently poor (for he possesses no wealth) but is in fact rich because he does not need wealth, preferring to live a simple life (cf. Chapter 9, 'The *Dervish* of the Kingdom of Birds', n. 8). The counsel of such a person is likely to be sincere and wise since in giving it he has no axe to grind.
[2]*Be a Fatimah . . . arms:* The words used for Fatimah and Husayn in the text are respectively 'Batul' and 'Shabbir'. Iqbal plays on Fatimah's nickname, Batul, for this word means literally one who leads a solitary life, having renounced worldly pleasures, and is devoted to the worship of God. Batul is also a name for the Virgin Mary.

SELF-PORTRAIT

In the quatrains, as in many other poems, Iqbal talks of himself—the uniqueness of his message, his regret at being appreciated for the wrong reasons, his confrontation with Western thought and culture, his love of the Prophet, and his concerns over the Muslim Community.

SAME MESSAGE, UNIQUE VISION

In my hands I hold the same old violin,[1]
Full of plaintive songs with many melodies.
But I play it with the claws of a lion,[2]
For its strings are made of gut as hard as rock.

AHF 859:2 [1015:1]

[1]*I hold . . . violin:* I present the same old message of Islam.
[2]*But I play . . . lion:* The message demands courage and determination in those who would live and order their lives by it. See next quatrain.

I do not know the birds in the garden,
On the branch where my nest is built I sing alone.
If you are weak of heart, stay away from me,
For my song drips blood.

PM 213:2 [205:2]

Two hundred sages spoke in this assembly,
Their words more delicate than jasmine petals.
But tell me, who is that keen-sighted man
Who saw a thorn and spoke of the garden?[1]

AHF 860:3 [1016:3]

[1]*But tell me . . . garden?* This could be read as a general question. On the other hand, Iqbal could be referring to his own ability to look at the wretched state ('the thorn') of the Muslim Community and talk either about the glorious Muslim civilisation of the past (for purposes of drawing a contrast) or the great future potential of this civilisation (for purposes of motivating people to action); the 'garden' would thus stand for either past glory or future prospects. The analogy that comes to mind is of an archeologist who, on the basis of a few finds, can form a detailed picture of the city to which they belong.

VERSATILE TALENT, CHECKERED FATE

I wish someone saw how I play the flute –
The breath is Indian, the tune Arabian!
My vision has a taint of the Western style;
I am a Ghaznavi by temper, but my fate is that of an Ayaz![1]

BJ 407:2 [374:2]

[1] *a Ghaznavi . . . fate:* Mahmud of Ghaznah (in Afghanistan) was a great conqueror; Ayaz was his slave. Iqbal is saying that he has the mind and disposition of a king but the lot of a slave.

UNAPPRECIATED – OR PRAISED FOR WRONG REASONS

In both East and West I am a stranger –
I am not blessed with intimate friends;
Of my sorrow I can only speak to my own heart –
How innocently I beguile my loneliness![1]

[1] *Of my . . . loneliness!* Being lonely, I try to create the impression of company by speaking of my sorrow to my heart – an innocent act of self-deception!

AHF 800:3 [933:3]

They did not discover the secret I had told them of;
They did not eat the fruit of my date-palm:
Lord of nations,[1] I petition you for justice –
My friends take me to be a singer of lyrics![2]

AHF 795:3 [925:2]

[1] *Lord of nations:* Muhammad.
[2] *My friends . . . lyrics!* People take me to be just another poet. The word for 'lyrics' in the original is *ghazal,* which ordinarily means 'love-song'.

When I packed up to leave this earth,
Everyone said, 'We knew him!'
But no one knew what this traveller said,
And to whom – and where he had come from.

AHF 863:1 [1021:1]

CONFRONTATION WITH MODERNITY

I broke the spell of modern learning:
I took away the bait and broke the trap.[1]
God knows with what indifference,
Like Abraham, I sat in its fire![2]

AHF 800:4 [934:1]

[1] *I took . . . trap:* Modern learning failed to ensnare me: like a clever bird I made away with the bait from under the trap without being caught.

[2] *God knows . . . fire!* A reference to Qur'an 21:68-69, where God causes the fire into which Abraham is thrown by his ruthless opponents to become 'cool and safe' for him. Iqbal says that he faced an ordeal similar to Abraham's: he was thrown into the 'fire' of modern learning (Iqbal was educated at some of the finest educational institutions of Europe), but was unharmed by it; like Abraham, he was saved from being 'burnt' because, like Abraham, he had strong faith.

Like Rumi[1] I made the prayer-call in the Ka^{c}bah;
And learned from him the secrets of the soul.
He was meant to take up the challenge of a past age;
I am meant to take up the challenge of this age.[2]

AHF 803:2 [938:2]

[1] *Rumi:* Jalaluddin Rumi of Anatolia (13th century), a distinguished Sufi master whose Persian poetry was one of Iqbal's chief inspirations.

[2] *He was . . . this age:* The word used in the original is *fitnah*, which means ordeal or trial. Rumi took up the challenge posed by rationalism in the medieval age of Islam; Iqbal will take up the challenge posed by the modern age of secular materialism.

LOVE OF THE PROPHET

In the ocean that has no shore
The heart is the lovers' only guide;
We set off for Mecca because you told us to,
Otherwise you alone are our destination![1]

AHF 797:2 [928:2]

[1] *We set off . . . destination!* We went to Mecca (where the Ka^{c}bah is) only because you – Muhammad – told us to, otherwise we would have been content

to live in Medina (your city). In other words, even God is known through Muhammad.

WILL THERE BE ANOTHER LIKE ME?

Will the old song return?
Will another breeze arrive from the Hijaz?[1]
The time of this *faqir*[2] has come –
Will there be another who knows all secrets?

AHF 775:3 [894:3]

[1]*the Hijaz:* Region in the Arabian peninsula that includes Mecca and Medina and adjoining areas; loosely, Arabia.

[2]*faqir:* Literally 'one who is poor and in want'. In Iqbal the word acquires different connotations: one who disdains the world, thinks nothing of worldly goods and glory, has a high degree of self-respect etc. (see Chapter 1, 'Do One of the Two!', n. 6). Iqbal is proud to call himself a *faqir.*

BETWEEN HOPE AND DESPAIR

ᶜAjam[1] became young again through my songs;
My frenzy raised the price of its wares.[2]
It was a crowd lost in the wilderness:
The sound of my bell made it a caravan.

PM 235:1 [241:3]

[1]*ᶜAjam:* Persia; but the wider meaning of 'the non-Arab world' is intended here.

[2]*My frenzy . . . wares:* Iqbal's passionate poetry, by which he sought to reawaken ᶜAjam, raised the price of ᶜAjam's wares – that is, gave new importance to ᶜAjam in the world.

My passion puts fire into the Muslim's veins,
And my restive tears drop from his eyes;
But still he is not aware of the tumult in my soul –
For he has not seen the world with my eyes.

PM 238:4 [247:3]

A WISH

Give to the youth my sighs of dawn;[1]
Give wings to these eaglets again.
This, dear Lord, is my only wish –
That my insights should be shared by all!

BJ 411:1 [378:1]

[1] *My sighs of dawn:* The prayer that arises, at dawn, from the depths of Iqbal's heart for the Muslim community (cf. Chapter 7, 'Petöfi', n. 2). 'Dawn' here alludes to the dawn prayer, the first of the five obligatory daily prayers.

RECOMMENDED READING

The following works are recommended for further study. For a fuller bibliography, which is old but still useful, see Annemarie Schimmel's book, below.

Anthologies of Iqbal's poetry

Kiernan, V. G., *Poems from Iqbal* (London: John Murray, 1955).

Matthews, D. J., *Iqbal: A Selection of the Urdu Verse – Text and Translation* (London: School of Oriental and African Studies, University of London, 1993).

Interpretation and criticism

Malik, Hafeez, ed., *Iqbal: Poet-Philosopher of Pakistan* (New York: Columbia University Press, 1971).

Schimmel, Annemarie, *Gabriel's Wing: A Study into the Religious Ideas of Sir Muhammad Iqbal* (Leiden: E. J. Brill, 1963; reprinted with new foreword, Iqbal Academy, Pakistan 1989).

Sheikh, Saeed, ed., *Studies in Iqbal's Thought and Art* (Lahore: Bazm-i Iqbal, 1972).

Singh, *Iqbal, The Ardent Pilgrim: An Introduction to the Life and Work of Mohammed Iqbal*, 2nd edn. (Delhi: Oxford University Press, 1997).

Vahid, Syed Abdul, *Iqbal: His Art and Thought* (London: John Murray, 1959).